BEFORE HE LONGS

(A MACKENZIE WHITE MYSTERY—BOOK 10)

BLAKE PIERCE

D1528193

ISBN: 978-1-64029-384-7

PROLOGUE

She was scared to open her eyes. She had closed them some time ago—how long, she didn't know—because she had been sure he was going to kill her. He hadn't, yet she was still unable to open her eyes. She did not want to see him or what he had in store for her. She hoped that when it came, her death would be a bit more painless if she wasn't aware of which method he used.

But with each minute that passed, Claire started to wonder if he had death on his mind at all. Her head was ringing from where he had hit her in the head with something. A hammer of some sort, she thought. The memory was murky, as was the memory of what had happened once he'd struck her on the head.

Even with her eyes closed, there were some things that Claire could deduce. At some point, he had placed her into the back seat of his car. She could hear the hum of the engine and the low volume of a local radio station (WRXS, playing only true and original grunge from the Seattle area). She could also smell something familiar, not a food smell but something organic.

Just open your eyes, stupid, she thought. *You know you're in a car and he's driving. He can't very well kill you now, can he?*

She willed herself to open her eyes. When she did, the car hit a small bump and started to slow down. She heard the low squeal of brakes and the crunching of gravel underneath the tires. "Love, Hate, Love" by Alice in Chains was on the radio. She saw the WRXS call letters in digital letters on the radio in front of her. She saw the shapes of the two seats between her and the man who had hit her in the head with the hammer.

Of course, there was also the fact that she was bound and gagged. She was pretty sure the thing he had put in her mouth and tightened around her cheeks was some sort of sex gag, complete with the red ball in the center. As for whatever was binding her arms together behind her back, it felt like some sort of nylon strap. She assumed that was the same thing tying her legs together at the ankles.

As if sensing she had opened her eyes, he turned around and faced her. He smiled at her and in that moment, she remembered why she had given in to him so easily. Psychotic or not, the man was handsome.

1

He turned back around and put the car in park. When he got out of the car and then opened the back door, he did so casually. It seemed like he did something like this every day. He reached in and grabbed her by the shoulders. When his right hand grazed harshly by her breast, she couldn't tell if it was intentional or not.

He pulled her toward him by the shoulders. She tried kicking at him but her bound ankles would not allow it. When she was in the open air and out of the car, she saw that it was nearly dusk. It was sprinkling rain—not really sprinkling, but what her father had always referred to as *spitting*—and foggy.

Behind them, she saw his car and a slight hill. A small gravel driveway and a length of chain that extended to an old dilapidated doghouse in the yard. The doghouse looked odd…as if it had been constructed to look old. And there was something inside of it…not a dog at all but a…

What the hell is that? she wondered. But she knew what it was. And it creeped her out. Her fear ramped up and something about the weirdly placed object in the doghouse made her sure that she was going to die—that the man carrying her over his shoulder was completely out of his mind.

There was a doll in there. Two of them, maybe. It was hard to tell. They had been set up to face one another, their heads angled slightly.

It looked like they were gazing out of the opening of the doghouse, watching her.

A gnawing horror settled itself in her mind and refused to let go.

"What are you doing to me?" she asked. "Please…I'll do anything if you let me go."

"I know you will," he told her. "Oh, I know."

He stepped up onto a rickety porch step and made a harsh swinging gesture with his right shoulder. Claire barely felt the impact of the railing against the side of her head. The darkness came on far too fast for her to really register it at all.

***

She opened her eyes and knew that time had passed. Too much time.

And she had the feeling she was no longer at the house near that doghouse. She had been moved.

Her fear rocketed.

Where had he taken her now?

2

She cried out—and as soon as a moan left her mouth, he was there. His hand fell roughly on her mouth. He pressed himself against her. His breath smelled like old potato chips and everything about him from the waist down felt hard. She tried to fight against it but found that she was still tied up.

"It'll be okay," he said.

And with that, he kissed her on the mouth. It was a slow one, as if he was really savoring it. But there was also nothing lustful about it. Despite the obvious erection at her hip and the kiss itself, she could sense nothing at all sexual about what he was trying to do.

He stood up and looked down at her. He showed her the gag that had been in her mouth and applied it once more. She shook her head against it but he only pressed it down harder. When he dropped her head after attaching something in the back, it hit the floor.

Her eyes searched frantically for anything to help her and that's when she knew for sure she was not in his house. No…this was different. There were various odds and ends everywhere, stacked against metal walls. A dim light bulb hung overhead.

No, she thought. *Not his house. This is like one of those storage lockers…hell, is this* my *storage locker?*

That's exactly what it was. And this fact slammed into her brain harder than the floor had slammed into her back. It also made her fairly certain that she was indeed going to die after all.

He stood up and looked almost lovingly down at her. He smiled again and this time there was nothing handsome about him. Now he looked like a monster.

He walked away, opening a door that made an almost mechanical noise when it moved. He slammed it closed without another look at her.

In the darkness, Claire closed her eyes again and screamed against the ball gag in her mouth. It vibrated in her head until she thought her skull would crack in half. She screamed a silent scream until she could taste blood in her mouth, and sometime shortly after that, there was the darkness again.

CHAPTER ONE

Mackenzie White's life had become something she had never envisioned for herself. She had never been into nice clothes or caring about fitting into the popular crowd. While she was strikingly beautiful by most people's standards, she had never been what her father had once called "the prissy sort."

Yet lately, she had felt that way. She blamed it on planning the wedding. She blamed it on the wedding magazines and cake tastings. From one potential wedding location to the next, from ordering fancy invitations to trying to decide on the reception menu—she had never felt more like a stereotypical female in her entire life.

That's why when she took the sleek and familiar nine-millimeter in her hand, it was claiming. It was like returning to an old friend that knew who she really was. She smiled at the feeling as she stepped into the entryway of the bureau's new simulated active shooter arena. Based on the idea behind the infamous Hogan's Alley—a tactical training facility designed to look like any urban street and used by the FBI ever since the late '80s—the new arena boasted state of the art equipment and new obstacles that most agents and agents-in-training had yet to experience. Among the equipment were robotic target arms equipped with infrared lights that worked much the same way as laser tag. If she did not down a target fast enough, the light on the arm would flash at her, triggering a small alarm on the vest she was wearing.

She thought of Ellington and how he had referred to it as the bureau's take on *American Ninja Warrior.* And he wasn't too far off as far as Mac was concerned. She looked up to the red light in the corner of the entryway, waiting for it to turn green. When it did, Mackenzie did not waste a single moment.

She entered the arena and instantly started looking for targets. The place was set up almost like a video game in that targets popped up from behind obstacles, corners, and even from the ceiling. They were all attached to robotic arms that remained hidden and, from what she understood, never popped the targets out in the same timed progression. Therefore, on this, her second time through, none of the targets she had downed the first time would come out when it had the previous time. It would always present itself as a new course.

4

Two steps in, a target came popping from behind a strategically placed crate. She popped it down with a round from the nine-millimeter and instantly started strafing forward looking for more. When it came, it came from the ceiling, a target roughly the size of a softball. Mackenzie put a round directly through its center as another target came from the right. She blasted through this one as well and continued into the room.

To say this was cathartic was an understatement. While she did not resent the wedding planning and the direction her life was taking, there was still some kind of freedom in allowing her body to move instinctually, reacting to intense situations. Mackenzie had not been part of an active case in nearly four months now, focusing on closing up the few loose ends in her father's case and, of course, the upcoming wedding with Ellington.

During that time, she had also gotten something of a promotion. While she still worked under Director McGrath and reported directly to him, she had been tasked with becoming something of his go-to agent. It was another reason she had not worked actively on any case in nearly four months; McGrath was busy trying to determine just what role he wanted her to play within the pool of agents under his watchful eye.

Mackenzie moved through the course like something mechanical, like a robot that had been programmed to do this very thing. She moved fluidly, she aimed with precision and speed, she ran expertly and without hesitation. If anything, the four months parked behind a desk and in meetings had given her more motivation to take part in these kinds of training exercises. When she *did* get back out into the field, she fully intended to be a better agent than the one who had finally wrapped up her father's case.

She came to the end of the arena without really being aware that she was done. A large rolling metal door sat in the wall ahead of her. When she crossed the yellow line along the concrete of the arena that signified she was done, the door rolled upward. She then stepped into a small room with a table and a single monitor on the wall. The screen on the monitor showed her results. Seventeen targets, seventeen hits. Of the seventeen hits, nine were bull's-eye hits. Of the other eight, five were within twenty-five percent accuracy of being bull's-eyes. The overall rating for her course run was eighty-nine percent. It was five percent better than her previous run and nine percent better than any of the other one hundred nineteen results posted by other agents and trainees.

Need more practice, she thought as she exited the room and headed for the changing room. Before changing, she took her cell

5

phone out of her backpack and saw that she had a text from Ellington.

Mom just called. She'll be here a little early. Sorry…

Mackenzie sighed deeply. She and Ellington were seeing a possible venue for the wedding today and had decided to invite his mother. It would be the first time Mackenzie had ever met her and she felt like she was in high school again, hoping to live up to the scrutinizing eye of a watchful and loving mother.

Funny, Mackenzie thought. *Exceptional gun skills, nerves of steel…and still afraid of meeting my future mother-in-law.*

This domesticated-life stuff was really starting to irritate her. Still, she felt that stirring of excitement as she changed into her street clothes. They were going to see the venue of her choice today. They were getting married in six weeks. It was time to be excited. And with that in mind, she headed back home with a smile on her face most of the way.

***

As it turned out, Ellington was just as nervous about Mackenzie meeting his mom as Mackenzie was. When she returned to his apartment, he was pacing in the kitchen. He didn't look worried per se, but there was a nervous tension to the way he moved.

"You look scared," Mackenzie said as she took a seat on one of the barstools.

"Well, it just occurred to me that we'll be seeing this venue with my mother exactly two weeks after my divorce was finalized. Now, you and I and most rational human beings know that these things take a while because of paperwork and the snail-like pace of the government. But my mother…I guarantee you she's hanging on to this little bit of information, just waiting to spring it on me at a very bad time."

"You know, you're supposed to make me *want* to meet this woman," Mackenzie said.

"I know. And she's lovely most of the time. But she can be…well, a bitch when she wants to be."

Mackenzie got up and wrapped her arms around him. "That's her right as a woman. We all have it, you know."

"Oh, I know," he said with a smile and kissed her on the lips. "So…you ready for this?"

6

"I've put away killers. I've been in some high-octane chases and have stared down the barrels of countless guns. So…no. No, I'm not ready. This scares me."

"Then we'll be scared together."

They left the apartment in the casual way they had been doing ever since they had moved in together. For all intents and purposes, Mackenzie already felt like she was married to the man. She knew everything about him. She had gotten used to his light snoring and even his tendency toward '80s glam metal. She was starting to truly love the little touches of gray he was already getting along the base of his temples.

She'd been through hell with Ellington, encountering some of her tougher cases with him by her side. So surely they'd be able to tackle marriage together—temperamental in-laws and all.

"I have to ask," Mackenzie said as they got into his car. "Do you feel any lighter now that the divorce is final? Can you feel the space where that monkey used to be on your back?"

"It does feel lighter," he said. "But that was a pretty heavy monkey."

"Should we have invited her to the wedding? Seems your mom might have appreciated that."

"One of these days, I'll find you funny. I promise."

"I hope so," Mackenzie said. "It'll be a long life together if you keep missing my comedic genius."

He reached out and took her hand, beaming at her as if they were a couple who had just fallen in love. He drove them toward the venue where she was pretty sure they were getting married, both of them so happy that they could practically see the future, bright and shining just ahead of them.

CHAPTER TWO

Quinn Tuck had one simple dream: to sell the contents of some of these abandoned storage units to some schmuck like the ones he saw on that show *Storage Wars*. There was decent money in what he did; he brought home almost six grand every month on the storage units he maintained. And after knocking the mortgage on his house out last year, he'd been able to save just enough to be able to take his wife to Paris—something she hadn't shut up about since they'd started dating twenty-five years ago.

Really, he'd love to sell the whole place and just move away somewhere. Maybe somewhere in Wyoming, a place no one ever yearned for but was still fairly scenic and inexpensive. But his wife would never go for that—although she'd probably be happy if he got out of the storage unit business.

First of all, most of the clients were pretentious dicks. They were, after all, the types of people who had so many belongings that they had to rent extra space to store it all in. And second of all, she wouldn't miss the random calls on a Saturday from finicky unit owners, complaining of some of the dumbest things. This morning's call had come from an older woman who rented two units. She'd been taking things out of one of her units and claimed to have smelled something awful coming from one of the units near hers.

Usually, Quinn would say he'd check it out but do nothing. But this was a tricky situation. He'd had a similar complaint two years ago. He waited three days to check it out only to find that a raccoon had somehow managed to get into one of the units but not get back out. When Quinn found it, it had bloated and swollen up, dead for at least a week.

And that's why he was pulling his truck into the lot of his primary unit space on a Saturday morning instead of sleeping in and trying to coax some mid-morning sex out of his wife with promises of that Paris trip. This storage unit complex was his smaller one. It was an outdoor complex with fifty-four units in all. The rent for these was on the lower end and all but nine of them were rented out.

Quinn got out of his truck and walked out among the units. Each square of units contained six storage spaces, all the same size. He walked to the third block of units and realized that the woman who had called this morning had not been overdramatic. He could smell something wretched as well and the storage unit in question was still two whole units away. He took out his keyring and started cycling through them all until he came to the one for Unit 35.

By the time he got to the door of the unit, he was nearly afraid to open it. Something smell *bad.* He started to wonder if someone, somehow, had accidentally trapped their dog inside without knowing it. And somehow, no one had heard it barking and whimpering to get out. It was an image that stripped away all of Quinn's thoughts of getting freaky with his wife on a Saturday morning.

Wincing from the smell, Quinn inserted the key into the lock of Unit 35. When the lock popped open, Quinn removed it from the latch and then rolled the accordion-style door up.

The odor hit him so strongly that he took two heavy steps back, fearing he might actually puke. He held his hand to his mouth and nose, taking one small step forward.

But that's the only step he took. He saw what the smell was coming from by simply standing outside of the unit.

There was a body on the floor of the unit. It was up close to the front, a few feet away from the stacked things in the back—small lockers, cardboard boxes, and milk crates filled with a little of everything.

The body was a woman who looked to be in her early twenties. Quinn could not see any clear wounds on her, but there was a fair amount of blood puddled around her. It had gone beyond wet or sticky, having dried on the concrete floor.

She was pale as a sheet and her eyes were wide and unblinking. For a moment, Quinn thought she was staring right at him.

He felt a little cry rise up in his throat. Backing away before it could escape, Quinn dug his phone out of his pocket and called 911. He wasn't even sure if that was who you called for something like this but it was all he could think to do.

As the phone rang and the dispatcher answered, Quinn tried to back away but found himself unable to take his eyes off of the grisly sight, his gaze locked with that of the dead woman in the unit.

CHAPTER THREE

Neither Mackenzie nor Ellington wanted a big wedding. Ellington claimed he had gotten all of the wedding nonsense out of his system with his first marriage but wanted to make sure Mackenzie got everything she wanted. Her own tastes were simple. She would have been perfectly happy in a basic church. No bells, no whistles, no fabricated elegance.

But then Ellington's father had called them shortly after they had gotten engaged. His father, who had never really been part of Ellington's life, congratulated him but also informed him that he'd be unable to attend any wedding that Ellington's mother was at. He did, however, compensate for his future absence by connecting with a very wealthy friend in DC and booking the Meridian House for them. It was an almost obscene gift but it had also put an end to the question of when to marry. As it turned out, that answer was four months after the engagement, thanks to Ellington's father booking a particular date: September 5th.

And while that day was still two and a half months away, it felt much closer than that when Mackenzie stood in the gardens adjacent to the Meridian House. The day was perfect and everything about the place seemed to have been recently touched up and landscaped.

I'd marry him right here tomorrow if I could, she thought. As a rule, Mackenzie typically didn't give in to overly girly impulses but something about the idea of getting married here made her feel a certain way—somewhere between romantic and absolutely geeking out. She loved the old-world feel of the place, the simple warm charm and the gardens.

As she stood and took the place in, Ellington approached her from behind and placed his arms around her waist. "So…yeah, this is the place."

"Yeah, it is," she said. "We need to tell your father thank you. Again. Or maybe just un-invite your mother so he will show up."

"It might be a bit too late for that," Ellington said. "Especially since that's her, walking up the sidewalk to our right."

Mackenzie looked in that direction and saw an older woman whom the years had been kind to. She was wearing black sunglasses that made her look exceptionally young and sophisticated in a way that was nearly annoying. When she spotted

Mackenzie and Ellington standing in between two large beds of flowers and shrubs, she waved with a little too much enthusiasm.

"She looks sweet," Mackenzie said.

"So do candy bars. But have enough of them and they'll rot your   teeth." Mackenzie couldn't help but snicker at this, biting it down as Ellington's mother joined them.

"I'm hoping you're Mackenzie," she said.

"I am," Mackenzie said, unsure of how to take the joke.

"Of course you are, dear," she said. She gave Mackenzie a lazy hug and a bright smile. "And I'm Frances Ellington…but only because it's too much of a hassle to get my last name changed."

"Hello, Mother," Ellington said, stepping in to hug her.

"Son. My oh my, how on earth did you two manage to nail this place down? It's positively gorgeous!"

"I've worked in DC long enough to make friends with the right people," Ellington lied.

Mackenzie cringed inside. She absolutely understood why he felt the need to lie, but also felt at odds with being part of such a huge one involving her mother-in-law-to-be at this stage of their relationship.

"But not people that could help expedite the paperwork and legal ramifications of your divorce, I take it?"

It was a comment made with a bit of a sarcastic tone, meant to be a joke. But Mackenzie had interrogated enough people and knew enough about behaviors and facial twitches to know when someone was simply being cruel. Maybe it *was* a joke, but there was also some truth and bitterness to it.

Ellington, though, took in stride. "Nope. Haven't made friends like that. But you know, Mom, I'd really rather focus on today. On Mackenzie—a woman who isn't going to run me through the mud like the first wife you seem to be hung up on."

My God, this is terrible, Mackenzie thought.

She had to make a decision right there and then, and she knew it might affect her future mother-in-law's opinion of her, but she could deal with that later. She was about to make a comment, to excuse herself so that Ellington and his mother could have this tense conversation in private.

But then her phone rang. She checked it and saw McGrath's name. She took it as the opportunity she needed, holding the phone close to her and stating: "So sorry, but I need to take this."

11

Ellington gave her a skeptical look as she walked a bit further down the sidewalk. She answered the call as she hid herself behind some elaborate rose bushes.

"This is Agent White," she answered.

"White, I need you to come in. You and Ellington both, I think. There's a case I need to stick you two on ASAP."

"Are you in the office right now? On a Sunday?"

"I wasn't. But this call brought me here. When can the two of you be here?"

She grinned and looked to Ellington, still bickering with his mother. "Oh, I think we can make it pretty quickly," she said.

CHAPTER FOUR

Being Sunday, there was no one at the desk in the small waiting area outside of McGrath's office. In fact, his office door was standing open when Mackenzie and Ellington arrived. Mackenzie knocked on the door before entering anyway, knowing what a stickler McGrath could be when it came to privacy.

"Come on in," McGrath called out.

When they entered, they found McGrath behind his desk, rummaging through several folders. Papers were strewn everywhere and his desk looked to be in a mild state of chaos. Seeing a usually tidy McGrath in such a state made Mackenzie wonder just what sort of case had managed to fluster him this much.

"I appreciate you coming so quickly," McGrath said. "I know you're using most of your free time to plan the wedding."

"Hey, you tore me away from my mother," Ellington said. "I'll tackle whatever case you throw at me."

"That's good to hear," McGrath said, selecting a pile of paper-clipped papers from the clutter on his desk and tossing it to him. "Ellington, when you first started as a field agent, I had you working cleanup in a case in Salem, Oregon. A deal with the storage units. You remember it?"

"I do, actually. Five bodies, all turned up dead in storage units. No killer was ever found. It was assumed that when the FBI got involved, he got scared and stopped."

"That's the one. There's been an ongoing search for the guy but it's come up with nothing. And it's been the better part of eight years."

"Did someone finally find him?" Ellington asked. He was looking through the papers McGrath had handed him. Mackenzie caught a peek as well and saw a few reports and details from the Oregon murders.

"No. But bodies have started to show up in storage units again. This time in Seattle. One was found last week, which could be ruled as coincidence. But a second was found yesterday. The body had been dead for a while—at least four days from the looks of it."

"So then it's fairly safe to say that the cases in Seattle are no longer being considered isolated incidents?" Mackenzie speculated.

"That's right. So the case is yours, White." McGrath then turned to Ellington. "I don't know about sending you, though. I'd

13

like to because you two manage to work well together despite the relationship. But this close to the wedding…"

"It's your call, sir," Ellington said. Mackenzie was rather surprised by how flippant he was being about the call. "But I do think my history with the Oregon case could benefit Macken— Agent White. Plus, two heads and all of that…"

McGrath contemplated it for a moment, looking back and forth between the two of them. "I'll allow it, but this might very well be the final case the two of you are partnered on. I already have enough people uneasy with an engaged couple working together. Once you're married, you can forget about it."

Mackenzie understood this and even thought it was a good idea in principle. She nodded along with McGrath's explanation as she took the papers from Ellington's hand. She didn't take the time to read them right there, not wanting to appear rude. But she scanned them just enough to get the gist.

Five bodies had been discovered in storage units in 2009, all found within a span of ten days. One of the bodies seemed to have been killed rather recently while one had been killed so long before its discovery that the flesh had started to rot from its bones. Three suspects had been brought in but were ultimately cleared thanks to alibis and a lack of any real evidence.

"Of course, we're also not prepared to say there's a direct link between the two, right?" she asked.

"No, not yet," McGrath said. "But that's one of the things I'd like you to figure out. Look for connections while trying to find this guy."

"Anything else?" Ellington asked.

"No. Transportation is being handled as we speak, but you should be in the air within four hours. I'd really like this wrapped up before this maniac can net another five people like he did before."

"I thought we weren't saying there's a direct link," Mackenzie said.

"Not officially, no," McGrath said. And then, as if unable to help himself, he smirked and turned to Ellington. "You get to live with that sort of scrutiny for the rest of your life?"

"Oh yeah," Ellington said. "And I look forward to it."

***

They were halfway back to his apartment before Ellington bothered calling his mother. He explained that they had been called

14

away and asked if she would like to try to get together sometime after they got back. Mackenzie listened closely, barely able to hear his mother's reply. She said something about the perils of a romantic couple working together *and* living together. Ellington cut her off before she could really get going.

When he ended the call, Ellington tossed his phone on the floorboard and sighed. "So, Mom sends her best."

"I'm sure."

"But the thing she said about husband and wife also working together…you prepared for that?"

"You heard McGrath," she said. "That won't happen after we're married."

"I know. But still. We'll be in the same building, hearing about each other's cases. There are days where I think that would be awesome…but others when I wonder just how weird it could get."

"Why? You afraid I'm going to eventually overshadow you?"

"Oh, you already have," he said with a smile. "You just refuse to acknowledge it."

As they rushed to the apartment and then through the chore of packing, the reality of the situation hit her for the first time. This could be the last case she and Ellington ever worked on together. She was sure that they would look back on their cases together fondly when they got older, almost as a sort of inside joke. But for now, with the wedding still looming and two dead bodies waiting on the other side of the country, it was felt daunting—like the end of something special.

I guess we'll just have to go out with a bang, she thought as she packed her bag. She peeked over at Ellington, also packing a bag for the trip, and smiled. Sure, they were about to head into a potentially dangerous case and lives were likely on the line, but she couldn't wait to get on the road with him one more time…perhaps one *last* time.

15

CHAPTER FIVE

They arrived in Seattle with two crime scenes to visit: the location of the first victim, discovered eight days ago, and the location of the second victim, discovered just the day before. Mackenzie had never visited Seattle before so she was almost disappointed to see that one of the city's stereotypes appeared to very much be true: it was drizzling rain when they landed at the airport. The drizzle held up until they were in their rental car and then grew to a steady pour as they headed out to Seattle Storage Solution, the location of the most recently discovered body.

When they arrived, there was a middle-aged man waiting for them in his pickup truck. He stepped out, unlatched an umbrella, and greeted them at their car. He handed them another umbrella with a lopsided smile.

"No one from out of town really ever thinks to bring one," he explained as Ellington took it. He popped it up and, as chivalrous as ever, made sure Mackenzie was fully underneath it.

"Thanks," Ellington said.

"Quinn Tuck," the man said, offering his hand.

"Agent Mackenzie White," Mackenzie said, taking the offered hand. Ellington did the same, introducing himself as well.

"Come on, then," Quinn said. "No sense in putting it off. I'd rather be home, if it's all the same to you. The body's gone, thank Jesus, but the unit still gives me the heebie jeebies."

"Is this the first time you've ever had something like this happen before?" Mackenzie asked.

"It's the first thing this *terrible*, sure. I had a dead raccoon caught in a unit one time. And this other time, wasps somehow got into a unit, made a nest, and dive bombed the renter. But yeah…nothing this bad before."

Quinn brought them to a unit with a black **35** plastered above the garage-style door. The door was open and a policeman was milling around in the back of the unit. He carried a pen and notepad, jotting down something as Mackenzie and Ellington entered.

The policeman turned to them and smiled. "You folks with the bureau?" he asked.

"We are," Ellington said.

"Pleased to meet you. I'm Deputy Paul Rising. I thought I'd be out here when you arrived. I'm taking notes on everything stored in

16

here, hoping to find some sort of clues. Because as of right now, there's exactly none."

"Were you on the scene when the body was removed?"

"Unfortunately. It was pretty gruesome. A woman named Claire Locke, age twenty-five. She'd been dead for at least a week. It's not clear if she starved to death or bled out first."

Mackenzie slowly took in the sight of the unit. The back was stocked with boxes, milk crates, and several old trunks—typical things to be found in a storage unit. But the bloodstain on the floor made it quite different indeed. It wasn't a very large one, but she guessed it could have resulted in enough blood loss to lead to death. Perhaps it was her imagination, but she was pretty sure she could still smell some of the stench the body had left behind.

While Deputy Rising went on about his business with the boxes and bins in the back, Mackenzie and Ellington started to investigate the rest of the interior. As far as Mackenzie was concerned, a bloodstain on the floor pointed to something else worth finding. As she looked around for any clues, she listened to Ellington as he asked Rising about the case details.

"Was the woman bound or gagged in any way?" Ellington asked.

"Both. Hands tied behind her back, ankles tied together, and one of those ball gags in her mouth. The blood you see on the floor there came from a small stab wound high in her stomach."

Being bound and gagged at least explained why Claire Locke had been unable to make any noise to alert people on the other side of the unit walls. Mackenzie tried to imagine a woman locked in this crammed little space with no light, food, or water. It pissed her off.

As she slowly made a circuit around the unit, she came to the corner of the doorway. Rain drummed down in front of her, slapping at the concrete outside. But just along the inside of the metal door frame, Mackenzie spotted something. It was very low to the ground, at the very base of the frame that allowed the door to slide up and down.

She dropped to her knees and leaned in closer. When she did, she saw a splotch of blood on the edge of the groove. Not much…so little, in fact, that she doubted any of the cops had seen it yet. And then, on the floor just beneath the splotch of blood, was something small, ragged, and white.

Mackenzie gently touched it with her finger. It was piece of a torn fingernail.

Somehow, Claire Locke had managed to try to escape. Mackenzie closed her eyes for a moment, trying to envision it. Depending on how her hands had been tied, she could have backed up to the door, knelt down, and tried lifting the door upward. It would have been a futile attempt due to the lock outside, but certainly worth trying if you were on the verge of starving or bleeding to death.

Mackenzie waved Ellington over and showed him what she had found. She then turned to Rising and asked: "Do you recall if there were any additional injuries to Ms. Locke's hands?"

"Yes, actually," he said. "There were a few superficial cuts on her right hand. And I think most of one of her fingernails was missing."

He came over to where Mackenzie and Ellington were standing and let out a little *"Oh."*

Mackenzie continued looking but found nothing more than a few stray hairs. Hairs she assumed would belong to either Claire Locke or the owner of the unit.

"Mr. Tuck?" she said.

Quinn was standing just outside of the unit, perched under his umbrella. He was doing everything he could to not be standing in the unit—to not even be looking inside. At the sound of his name, though, he stepped inside reluctantly.

"Who does this unit belong to?"

"That's the fucked up part," he said. "Claire Locke had been renting this unit out for the last seven months."

Mackenzie nodded as she looked to the back, where Locke's belongings were stacked to the ceiling in neat little rows. The fact that it was her storage unit did add a degree of eeriness to it, but, she thought, might work to their advantage in eventually establishing motive or even tracking down the killer.

"Are there security cameras around here?" Ellington asked.

"I just have one right up at the front entrance," Quinn Tuck said.

"We've watched all of the footage from the last few weeks," Deputy Rising said. "There's nothing out of the ordinary. Currently, we're speaking to everyone who showed up here anytime during the last two weeks. As you can imagine, it's going to be tedious. We still have a dozen or so people to question."

"Any chance we could get our hands on that footage?" Mackenzie asked.

"Absolutely," Rising said, though his tone indicated that she was nuts to want to go fishing through it.

Mackenzie followed Ellington to the back of the unit. Part of her wanted to rummage through the boxes and bins but she knew it would likely not lead to much of anything. Once they had leads or potential suspects, they *may* find something worthwhile but until then, the contents within the unit would mean nothing to them.

"Is the body still with the coroner?" Mackenzie asked.

"To the best of my knowledge," Rising said. "Want me to call and let them know you're coming?"

"Please. And see what you can do about getting us that video footage."

"Oh, I can send that, Agent White," Quinn said. "It's all digital. Just let me know where you want me to send it."

"Come on," Rising said. "I'll lead you to the coroner's office. It's just happens to be two floors below my office."

With that, the four of them exited the storage unit and walked back out into the rain. Even under the umbrella, it was loud. It came down slow but hard, as if trying to wash away the sights and smells the unit had seen.

CHAPTER SIX

As it turned out, Quinn Tuck was extremely helpful. It seemed he wanted to get to the bottom of what had happened just as badly as anyone. That's why, when Mackenzie and Ellington got to the police station, he had provided a link for them to access all of his digital files from the security system at the storage complex.

They decided to start with the security footage rather than the body of Claire Locke. It gave them a chance to sit down and somewhat collect their bearings. It was nearing nightfall now and the rain was still coming down. As Deputy Rising got them set up with a monitor, Mackenzie looked back on the day and found it hard to believe that she had been standing in a picturesque garden and thinking about her wedding less than nine hours ago.

"Here are the relevant time stamps," Rising said, slipping Mackenzie a piece of paper from his notepad. "There aren't many." He tapped his finger at one entry in particular, written in slanted handwriting. "This is the only time we see Claire Locke enter the complex. We pulled her DMV info and got her license plate number, so we know it's her. And this," he said, tapping at another entry, "is when she left. And these are the only times she shows up on the footage."

"Thanks, Deputy," Ellington said. "This helps tremendously."

Rising gave a little nod of acknowledgment before backing out of the tiny spare office the agents had been given. The monotonous work took a while, but as Rising had indicated, the local PD had already done some of the work for them. They were able to fast-track the footage when there was no activity on the screen. They started by checking the time stamps on the sheet of paper. When the car said to belong to Claire Locke came onto the screen, Mackenzie zoomed in but was unable to see a driver. She waited, watching the featureless entrance of the complex for twenty-two sped up minutes before Locke's car was shown leaving. In the time she had spent there, no one else had arrived and no other cars had left.

"You know," Mackenzie said, "it's entirely possible that she was not attacked *at* the storage unit."

"You think someone killed her elsewhere and brought her to the site?"

"Maybe not *killed* her somewhere else, but potentially abducted her. I think seeing her body will help determine that. If she shows signs of starvation or dehydration, that basically *tells* us that she was dumped there."

"But according to the report, the lock was bolted from the outside."

"So maybe someone else has the key," Mackenzie suggested.

"Probably someone in one of the other cars on these days and days of footage."

"Most likely."

"You want to stay here and roll through this while I go check out the body?" Ellington asked. "Or the other way around?"

Mackenzie pictured the poor woman, alone in the dark and unable to so much as scream for help. She envisioned her stumbling in the dark to try to find some way to at least try to get that door open.

"I think I'd like to check the body. You good here?"

"Oh yeah. This is streaming at its finest. No commercials or anything."

"Good," she said. "See you in a bit."

She leaned down and kissed him on the side of the mouth before leaving. She did it naturally and without much thought, even though it wasn't the most professional thing. It was a good reminder of just why they wouldn't be able to work together in this capacity after they were married.

Mackenzie left the little office space in search of the morgue while Ellington watched time unroll in fast-forward motion on the screen.

***

The question as to whether or not Claire Locke had experienced starvation or dehydration of any degree during her time in the storage unit was answered the moment Mackenzie saw her. While Mackenzie was not an expert on the subject, there was a hollow look to the young woman's cheeks. There might have been a similar look to her stomach as well but it was not clear due to the incision the coroner had made.

The woman who met her at the morgue was a rotund and eerily pleasant woman named Amanda Dumas. She greeted Mackenzie warmly and stood back against a small steel table that was adorned with the tools of her trade.

"Based on your examination," Mackenzie said, "would you say that the victim experienced severe hunger or dehydration before she died?"

"Yes, though I don't know to what extent, exactly," Amanda said. "There's very little fatty acid in her stomach—hardly any at all. That, plus some signs of muscle deterioration, indicates that she experienced at least the first pangs of starvation. There are telltale signs of dehydration as well, though I can't be sure that either of those is what killed her."

"You think she bled out first?"
"I do. And quite frankly, that would have been a blessing for her."

"Based on what you've seen with the body, do you believe she was alive when she was placed in the storage unit?"

"Oh, without a doubt. And I'd say it was against her will as well." Amanda stepped forward and pointed to the abrasions on Locke's right hand. "Looks like she put up a fight of some kind and then tried her best to escape at some point."

Mackenzie saw the cuts and noted that one of them looked rather ragged. It could have easily been placed there by the grooved runner that the unit door ran within. She also saw the fingernail that had been torn.

"There's also bruising along the back of her head," Amanda said. She used a comb-like tool to move Claire's hair aside. She did so with a loving sort of respect and care. When she did this, Mackenzie was able to see an angry purple bruise along the upper base of her neck where her skull joined it.

"Any signs that she was drugged?" Mackenzie asked.

"None. I still have one chemical analysis I'm waiting on, but based on everything else I've seen, I'm not expecting anything from it."

Mackenzie assumed the bruise to the back of the head along with the ball gag found in her mouth was more than enough reason for Claire Locke to not have raised any fuss or alarm when she was carried into the storage unit. She thought about the video footage again, certain that the driver of one of the cars was responsible for her murder—and the death of the other person found last week, according to the reports.

Mackenzie looked back down at the body with a frown. It was a natural reaction to always feel some sort of remorse for anyone who had been murdered. But Mackenzie was feeling a stronger sense of sadness with Claire Locke. Maybe it was because she could picture her all alone in that dark storage unit, unable to properly move or call out for help.

"Thanks for the information," Mackenzie said. "My partner and I will be in town for a few days. Let me know if anything shows up in that last chemical report."

She left the morgue and headed back up to the main floor. On her way back to the little office she and Ellington were working out of, she stopped by the dispatch desk and requested a copy of the current file on Claire Locke. She had it in her hands two minutes later and carried it back to the office.

She found Ellington staring at the monitor, reclined back in his chair.

"Anything so far?" she asked.

"Nothing concrete. I've watched seven more vehicles come and go. One stayed for about six hours before leaving. I want to check with the PD to see which of these people they have already spoken with. For Claire Locke to end up in that storage unit, someone on this footage had to have driven her there."

Mackenzie nodded in agreement as she started looking through the file. Locke had no criminal record at all and the personal details didn't offer much. She was twenty-five years old, graduated from UCLA two years ago, and had been working as a digital artist with a local marketing firm. Divorced parents, the father living in Hawaii and the mother somewhere in Canada. No husband, no kids, but there was a note along the bottom of the personal details sheet that stated her boyfriend had been informed of her death. He'd been called yesterday at three in the afternoon.

"How much time do you have left on that?" she asked.

Ellington shrugged. "Three more days, it looks like."

"You good here while I head out to speak to Claire Locke's boyfriend?"

"I guess," he said with a comical sigh. "Married life is coming up. Better get used to seeing me sitting in front of a screen all the time. Especially during football season."

"That's fine," she said. "As long as you're fine with me heading out and doing my own thing while you're doing it."

And to show him what she meant, she headed back out. She called over her shoulder: "Give me a few hours."

"Sure thing. But don't expect dinner to be ready when you get back."

The banter between them made her incredibly happy that McGrath had allowed them to work this case together. Between the gloom and rain outside and her peculiar sadness toward Claire Locke, she didn't know if she would have been able to properly handle this case on her own. But with Ellington here, she felt that she had a piece of home with her—somewhere to return in the event the case got too overwhelming.

She headed back outside. Night had fallen and although the rain had once again settled down to a lazy drizzle, Mackenzie couldn't help but feel that it was an omen of sorts.

CHAPTER SEVEN

Mackenzie knew nothing about the boyfriend, as there was nothing about him in the notes. All she knew was that his name was Barry Channing and that he lived at 376 Rose Street, Apartment 7. When she knocked on the door of Apartment 7, it was answered by a woman who looked to be in her late fifties or so. She looked tired and saddened—and clearly not happy to have a visitor after nine o'clock on a rainy Sunday night.

"Can I help you?" the woman asked.

Mackenzie nearly double-checked the number on the door but instead stated, "I'm looking for Barry Channing."

"I'm his mother. Who are you?"

Mackenzie showed her ID. "Mackenzie White, with the FBI. I was hoping to ask him some questions about Claire."

"He's really in no state to talk to anyone," the mother said. "In fact, he—"

"My God, Mom," a male voice said, coming toward the door. "I'm okay."

The mother stepped aside, making room for her son to stand in the doorway. Barry Channing was rather tall and had close-cropped blond hair. Like his mother, he looked low on sleep and it was clear that he had been crying.

"You said you're with the FBI?" Barry said.

"Yes. Do you have a few minutes?"

Barry looked at his mother with a small frown and then sighed. "Yes, I have some time. Come in, please."

Barry led Mackenzie into the apartment, down a thin hallway, and into a generic-looking kitchen. His mother, meanwhile, sulked on further down the hallway and out of sight. As Barry settled into a chair at the kitchen table, Mackenzie heard a door close rather forcefully from somewhere else in the apartment.

"Sorry about that," Barry said. "I'm starting to think my mother was closer to Claire than I was. And that's saying a lot, seeing as how I purchased an engagement ring two weeks ago."

"I'm very sorry for your loss," Mackenzie said.

"I've been hearing that a lot," Barry said, looking at the tabletop. "It was unexpected and while I did cry like a baby when the police told me yesterday, I'm managing to keep it together. Mom came over to stay with me to help me get through the funeral

25

and I'm thankful for her help, but she's a little overprotective. Once she's gone, I'll probably let all the grief out, you know?"

"I'm going to ask what might seem like a dumb question," Mackenzie said. "But do you know of anyone that might have any reason to do this to Claire?"

"No. The police asked the same thing. She didn't have any enemies, you know? She and her mother didn't get along, but it wasn't nearly to the level that would cause this. Claire was a sort of private person, you know? No close friends or anything…just acquaintances. That sort of thing."

"When did you see her last?" Mackenzie asked.

"Eight days ago. She came by here to see if I had anything I needed to put in her storage unit. We had a laugh over it. She didn't know I had the ring. But we both knew we were going to get married. We started making plans for it. Her asking if I had anything to put in her unit was just another way of reinforcing it, you know?"

"After that day, how long passed before you started to get frightened? I don't see where you filed a missing persons report or anything like that."

"Well, I'm taking classes at the community college, getting my GPA up to get back to college and finally finish. It's a huge workload and that's on top of a job where I put in forty to forty-five hours a week. So there would be four or five days that would go by where Claire and I wouldn't see one another. But after three days and no texts or calls, I did start to get worried. I went by her apartment to check on her and she didn't answer. I thought about calling the police, but it seemed stupid. And really, deep in the back of my head, I wondered if she had just up and left me. That maybe the whole idea of getting married had scared her or something."

"On that last time you saw her, did she seem okay? Was she acting out of the ordinary?"

"No, she was great. In a good mood."

"By any chance, do you know what she was going to the storage unit to store?"

"Probably some of her textbooks from college. She'd been carrying them around in her trunk for a while."

"Do you know how long she'd been renting that unit?"

"About six months. She was moving stuff from California and storing it. Again…we had this thing where we felt we were going to get married so instead of moving stuff straight into her apartment, she left some of it in the unit. It's why she rented it at all, I think. I told her she didn't need it but she kept saying how it would be so much easier when we moved in together."

"I asked about Claire having any enemies…but how about you? Is there anyone that would do this to hurt you?"

Barry looked stunned, as if he had never considered such a thing. He shook his head slowly and she thought he might start weeping. "No. But I almost wish there was. It would help to make sense of this. Because I just don't know anyone that would want Claire dead. She was just…she was very kind. The sweetest person you could ever meet."

Mackenzie could tell that he was being sincere. She also knew that she was not going to get anything out of Barry Channing. She placed one of her business cards on the table and slid it over to him.

"If you think of anything at all, please call me," she said.

He took the card and only nodded.

Mackenzie felt that she should say something else but it was one of those moments where it was clear that there was nothing more to say. She made her way to the door and as she closed it behind her she felt a pang of regret as she heard Barry Channing begin to cry.

The rain outside was little more than a mist now. As she walked back to her car, she called Ellington, hoping the rain would die out completely. She wasn't quite sure why it was bothering her so much. It just *did*.

"This is Ellington," he answered, never one to check his display before answering.

"You done with watching TV yet?"

"I am, actually," he replied. "I'm working with Deputy Rising right now to cross off the people on the list that they've already spoken to. Anything new on your end?"

"No. But I want to go to the storage unit that the first body was found in. Can you get that information from Rising and meet me in front of the station in about twenty minutes? And see if someone can get the owner on the phone."

"Can do. See you then."

They ended the call and Mackenzie drove on, thinking of the grieving boyfriend she had left behind…thinking of Claire Locke, alone in the dark, starving and terrified in her last moments.

CHAPTER EIGHT

Mackenzie and Ellington arrived at U-Store-It at 10:10. The facility was different from Seattle Storage Solution in that it was an actual building. The structure itself looked as if it had once been a small warehouse of some kind but the exterior had been prettied up with simple landscaping that was only half revealed in the small lights that bordered the sidewalk. Because they called ahead, a light was on inside as the owner and manager of the place waited for them.

The owner met them at the door, a small and overweight man with glasses named Ralph Underwood. He seemed pleased to have them there and didn't make much of an attempt to hide the fact that he was quite taken with Mackenzie.

He led them through the front of the building, which consisted of a small waiting area and even smaller conference room. He'd done a good job of making the place look warm and cozy but it still had the smell of an old warehouse.

"How many units do you have here?" Ellington asked.

"One hundred and fifty," Underwood said. "Each unit has a door along the back so things can easily be loaded and unloaded from the outside rather than having to come in through the front of the building."

"Seems pretty efficient," Mackenzie said, never having seen a storage complex that was held totally within another building.

"You said on the phone you were interested in learning more about the body I found two weeks ago, correct?"

"That's right," Mackenzie said. She'd had Rising send her over the report and she read from it now, on her phone. "Elizabeth Newcomb, age thirty. According to the police report she was found in her own storage unit, dead due to a stab wound to the chest."

"I don't know about all of that," Underwood said. "All I know is that when I came in that morning and walked the grounds like I always do, I saw something red along the edge of the unit door. I knew what it was right away but tried to convince myself I was wrong. But when I unlocked the unit, there she was. Lying on the floor, dead, in a pool of blood."

He told the story as if he were sitting at a campfire. It irritated Mackenzie a little but she also knew that people with a bent toward the dramatic were often good sources of information.

"Ever find anything like that before?" Ellington asked.

"No. But I tell you...I've had about a dozen or so units abandoned. It's in my contract that if the unit has not been opened at least once within three months, I call the user just to make sure they're still interested in the space. If there has been no communication after six months, I sell the units at auction, belongings and all."

Mackenzie knew that this was a common practice but as far as she was concerned, it seemed nearly illegal.

"Some of the things people leave in these units are...well, disturbing," Underwood went on. "In three of the abandoned units I've had, there was all kinds of sex toys. Someone had fifteen guns in theirs, including two AK-47s. One unit apparently belonged to a taxidermist because there were four stuffed animals...and I'm not talking teddy bears, you know?"

Underwood took them through a door at the back of the little entrance wing. There was no transition after the door; they walked through and were standing in a very wide hallway. The floor was concrete and the ceiling sat about twenty feet overhead. Now, more than ever, Mackenzie was convinced the place had once indeed been a warehouse of some kind. The units were broken into clusters of five, each cluster broken by a hallway that ran to the side of the building both ways. The clusters were on each side of the building, set up in a way that, when you looked down the central middle hallway, there seemed to be no end to them. Now that they were inside, Mackenzie saw the depth and range of the place for what it was. The building was easily one hundred yards long.

"The unit you want to see is just right up here a bit," Underwood said. They walked along for about two minutes, Underwood going on and on about the odd collectibles he had found in some of the abandoned units, as well as treasures like mint condition toys, valuable comics, and one honest-to-God unopened safe that had more than five grand in it.

He finally brought them to a stop in front of a unit marked C-2. He had apparently pre-selected the key before their arrival; he dug a single key out of his pocket and unlocked the deadbolt lock on the door runner. He then slid the door up, revealing the musty inside. Underwood flicked a light switch on the wall and the light that shone down from the room revealed a mostly empty storage unit.

"No family has been by to claim her things?" Mackenzie asked.

"I got a call from her mother four days ago," he said. "She's coming by at some point, but she didn't set a date or anything."

Mackenzie walked around the unit, looking for anything that might look similar to what they had seen in Claire Locke's unit. But either Elizabeth Newcomb had not had the fighting spirit of Claire Locke or the evidence of her struggles had already been cleaned up by the PD and local detectives.

Mackenzie went to the few stacked belongings in the back. Most of them were in plastic bins, labeled with masking tape and black magic marker: **Books and Magazines, Childhood, Mom's Stuff, Christmas Decorations, Old Baking Stuff.**

Even the manner in which they were stacked seemed very organized. There were a few small cardboard boxes filled with photo albums and framed pictures. Mackenzie looked in a few of the albums but saw nothing that would help. She only saw pictures of smiling family members, beachfront vistas, and a dog that had apparently been a very cherished pet.

Ellington walked over to her and looked around at the boxes. He had his hands on his hips, one of his telltale indicators that he was at a loss. It still surprised her from time to time just how well she knew him.

"I think anything that might have been here to find was already found by the police," he said. "Maybe we can find something in the files."

Mackenzie was nodding, but her eyes had fallen on something else. She walked to the far corner, where three of the plastic storage bins had been stacked on top of one another. Tucked exactly in the corner, so far back that she had missed it during her initial inspection, was a doll. It was an older doll, its hair matted and little smudges of dirt on its cheeks. It looked like something that might have been stolen from the set of a cheesy horror movie.

"Creepy," Ellington said, tracing her gaze.

"And oddly out of place," Mackenzie said.

She picked the doll up, careful to keep her hands in one position on the back of it, just in case it might be some sort of clue. Sure, at first glance it seemed like just a random object in someone's storage bin—perhaps something thrown in at the last minute, as an afterthought.

But everything else in this unit is meticulously stacked and organized. This doll stands out. And not only that, it's almost as if it were meant to stand out.

"I think we need to bag it up," she said. "Why is this one object not boxed up and put away? This place is eerily neat. Why leave this out?"

"You think the killer placed it there?" Ellington asked. But before the question was fully out of his mouth, she could tell that he was considering it as a very real possibility as well.

"I don't know," she said. "But I think I want to go take another look at Claire Locke's unit again. And I also want to see how quickly we can get a full case file for the murders in Oregon that you worked on…back in the early days." She said the last bit with a smile, never missing an opportunity to tease him for being seven years older than she was.

Ellington turned back to Underwood. He was hanging out by the door, pretending not to eavesdrop. "I don't suppose you ever spoke with Ms. Newcomb outside of renting her the unit, did you?"

"Afraid not," Underwood said. "I try to be friendly and hospitable to everyone but there's just so many of them, you know?" He then eyed the doll Mackenzie still held and frowned. "Told you…lots of weird shit in these units."

Mackenzie didn't doubt it. But this particular weird item seemed sorely out of place. And she fully intended to find out what it meant.

CHAPTER NINE

Due to the late hour, Quinn Tuck had understandably been pissed off when Mackenzie had called. Still, he told them how to get into the complex and where the spare set of keys were. It was just before midnight when Mackenzie and Ellington opened up Claire Locke's storage unit again. Mackenzie couldn't help but feel that they were running in circles—not a feeling that was especially encouraging so early in the case—but she also felt that this was the right move.

With the doll from Elizabeth Newcomb's unit in mind, Mackenzie stepped back into the unit. Perhaps it was just being aware of the late hour, but the place seemed a bit more foreboding this time around. The bins and boxes stacked in the back weren't quite as perfect as the ones in Elizabeth Newcomb's unit, but they were still tidy.

"A little sad, isn't it?" Ellington said.

"What's that?"

"These things…these bins and boxes. Chances are no one who cares about what's inside of them will ever open them."

It *was* a sad thought, one that Mackenzie tried to push to the back of her mind. She walked to the back of the unit, feeling almost like an intruder. She and Ellington both checked over the contents for any dolls or other disturbances, but found nothing. It then occurred to Mackenzie that she was expecting to find something as obvious as a doll. Maybe there was something different, something smaller…

Or maybe there's no connection here at all, she thought.

"You see this?" Ellington asked.

He was kneeling next to the right wall. He nodded toward the corner of the unit, in a thin space between the wall and a stack of cardboard boxes. Mackenzie dropped down to her knees as well and saw what Ellington had spied.

It was a miniature teapot—not miniature as in a small teapot, but more like a playset teapot that little girls might use for an imagined tea time.

She crawled forward and picked it up off the floor. She was rather surprised to find that it was made not of plastic, but of a ceramic material. It felt just like a real teapot, only it was no bigger than six inches tall. She could set the entirety of the thing in her hand.

"If you ask me," Ellington said, "there's no way that was set there by accident or by someone just tired of packing shit into the unit."

"And it didn't just fall out of a box," Mackenzie added. "It's ceramic. If it had fallen from a box, it would have shattered on the floor."

"So what the hell does it mean?"

Mackenzie had no answer. They both looked to the little teapot, quite pretty but also dingy—just like the doll in Elizabeth Newcomb's unit. And despite its small size, Mackenzie felt that it represented something much larger.

***

It was 1:05 when they finally checked into a motel. Mackenzie was tired but also invigorated by the puzzle that the doll and the little teapot offered. Once in the room, she took a quick moment to change out of her work clothes and into a T-shirt and gym shorts. She powered up her laptop as Ellington changed into more comfortable clothes as well. She logged into her email and saw that McGrath had assigned someone to send them every single file they had on the Salem, Oregon, storage unit murders from eight years ago.

"What are you doing?" Ellington asked as he stepped up beside her. "It's late and tomorrow is going to be a long day."

Ignoring him, she asked: "Was there nothing in the Oregon cases that pointed to any of this? To a doll, a teapot…anything like that?"

"I honestly don't recall. Like McGrath said, I just ran cleanup. I questioned a few witnesses, tidied up reports and paperwork. If there was anything like that, it didn't stand out. I'm not ready to say the cases are linked. Yes, they are eerily similar, but not identical. Still…it might not hurt to eventually look into it. Maybe meet with the PD in Salem to see if anyone closer to the case remembers anything like that."

Mackenzie trusted his word but couldn't help but scan through several of the files before giving in to the need to sleep. She felt Ellington rest a hand on her shoulder and then felt his face next to hers.

"Am I being lazy if I turn in?"

"No. Am I being over-obsessive if I don't?"

"No. You're just being very dedicated to your job." He kissed her on the cheek and then fell into the room's single bed.

It was tempting to join him—not for any extracurricular activities, but to just enjoy some sleep before the frantic pace tomorrow would be sure to bring. But she felt that she had to find at least a few more potential pieces to the puzzle, even if they were buried in a case from eight years ago.

From a cursory glance, there was nothing to be found. There had been five people killed, all found in storage units. One of the units had contained more than ten thousand dollars' worth of valuable baseball cards and another had contained a macabre collection of medieval weaponry. Seven people had been questioned in regards to the deaths but none had ever been convicted. The theory the police and the FBI had worked with was that the killer was abducting his victims and then forcing them to open up their storage units. Based on the original reports, it did not appear as if the killer was stealing anything from the units, although it was obviously next to impossible to be certain of this.

From what Mackenzie could see, there were no peculiar items left behind at the scenes. The files contained pictures of the crime scenes and of the five victims, three of the storage units had been in a messy state, having not seen an obsessively organized touch like that of Elizabeth Newcomb.

Two of the crime scene images were strikingly clear. One was from the scene of the second victim, and the other from the fifth victim. Both units had been in a state of what Mackenzie thought of as organized chaos; there were piles of things here and there, but they were thrown together haphazardly.

Looking at the picture from the second crime scene, Mackenzie scoured the background, zooming in as much as she could without causing the screen to go all pixelated. Near the center of the room, on top of three precariously stacked boxes, she thought she saw something of interest. It looked like a pitcher of some kind, perhaps something to put water or lemonade in. It was sitting on what appeared to be a plate of some kind. While there were other random objects sitting out in the open, these appeared to have been placed with care in the very center of the room.

She stared until her eyes started to ache and could still not be certain what she was looking at. Knowing that it might be a long shot, she opened up an empty email to send directly to two agents she knew would act fast and efficiently—two agents whom, she randomly thought, she and Ellington needed to invite to their wedding: Agents Yardley and Harrison.

She attached the files she had received to the email and wrote a quick message: *Could either of you look into the files for these cases and see if anyone ended up taking an inventory of what was inside the storage units? Maybe check with the owners of the storage facilities.*

Knowing that there was very little left to do, Mackenzie finally allowed herself to go to bed. Because she was so tired and the day came falling down on her in a heap, she was asleep less than two minutes before her head hit the pillow.

Even when the eerie sight of the doll from Elizabeth Newcomb's storage unit surfaced in her head, she managed to ignore it—for the most part—and drift soundly to sleep.

CHAPTER TEN

Mackenzie wasn't at all surprised to wake up at 6:30 and find that Agent Harrison had come through. He was practically a research guru and had quickly learned his way around files, folders, and copious amounts of data. His email contained two attachments and a typical to-the-point message.

The two documents attached are inventories taken by the FBI. These are all we have because the families of two of the other victims refused bureau requests to go through their stored belongings. The fifth is missing because the owner of the facility auctioned the contents off three days after the death. Seems like a bastard thing to do, but the victim had no family to come collect her belongings.

I hope this helps. Let me know if you need anything more specific.

Mackenzie opened up the attachment and found a very simplified list prepared in a simple Word document. The first was seven pages long. The second was thirty-six pages long. The longer document was an inventory for a unit belonging to Jade Barker. The name clicked with Mackenzie instantly; she pulled up the crime scene images from the original documents and saw that the messier one had been Jade Barker's—the same one with the possible plate and pitcher sitting directly in the center of the image.

Mackenzie did a quick search through the document and found the two items listed on page two.

Toy pitcher.

Plastic toy plate.

Behind her, Ellington was getting dressed. As he buttoned up his shirt, he came over to her and looked at the screen. "Damn," he said. "They came through for you, didn't they?"

"Yes, they did," she said, pointing at the two items. She then considered something for a moment before asking: "Where exactly is Salem, Oregon?"

"Northern part of the state. I'm not sure where." He paused, looked at her with amused irritation, and sighed. "You planning on taking a day trip?"

"I think it might be worth it. I'd like to get a look at the sites and maybe speak to some of the family members."

"We have family members to speak with here," Ellington pointed out. "Starting with Elizabeth Newcomb's parents. And honestly, I'd like to have a chat with the policemen that originally went into that storage unit to get a detailed report."

"Sounds like you've got your morning planned out, then."

"Mac...Salem is like four hours away, I think. No sense in splitting up just so you can be on the road all damn day just to *hopefully* get a fuzzy idea of what happened out there eight years ago."

Mackenzie opened up a tab on her laptop and typed in *Seattle and Salem, OR*. Without looking back to him, she said: "It's three and a half hours...say three with me driving. If all goes smooth, I'll be back by dinner."

"If all goes smooth," Ellington echoed.

She smiled and stood up. "I love you, too."

With that, she kissed him and rather wished she *had* retired to bed a little earlier last night.

***

"Harrison, I need you to find some more information for me."

There was something about driving and speaking on the phone that exhilarated Mackenzie. Sure, she knew it was frowned upon but in her line of work, she saw it as the ultimate form of multitasking.

"And good morning to you, too," Agent Harrison said from the other end of the phone. "I take it you got my mail?"

"I did. And it was a tremendous help. But I was wondering if you could do some more digging for me."

She knew he would agree. In the past, he'd have to worry with what McGrath would think. But with Mackenzie's new role and position directly under McGrath, she knew that Harrison would push her request to the top of his pile.

"What do you need?"

"I'm heading toward Salem, Oregon, right now to get a look at the crime scenes and interview anyone that I can. I'd like for you to see if you can find the names and contact information for any family or close friends of the victims that live in the area."

"Yeah, I can get on that. How long of a drive are you looking at?"

"About three more hours."

"You'll have everything you need before you get there."

"Thanks, Harrison."

"So, is this case like some weird sort of pre-honeymoon thing for you two?" he asked.

"Far from it. I guess you could say it's sort of like foreplay," she joked.

"Yeah, that's too much information. Let me get back to work for you. Happy trails, Agent White."

They ended the call, leaving Mackenzie to stare out at Interstate 5 with nothing but her thoughts. She kept thinking about the image from the storage unit of Jade Barker, dead for about eight years. If the plate and pitcher she had spotted in the image were the same two objects that had been inventoried by the FBI, what did it mean? Sure, it was a thin connection to some weird findings in this new Seattle case, but where did it lead? Even if she left Salem with irrefutable proof that the killer was leaving behind tea party–themed trinkets and toys (and yes, she included dolls in a tea party theme), did it really accomplish much of anything?

Sure it does, she thought to herself. *It gives us a bizarre path to pursue. It lets us hone in on one specific feature of the crime scenes—a feature that apparently means something special to the killer.*

And there was one more thing, too. It would give them a glimpse into just how dangerous and warped this killer could be.

CHAPTER ELEVEN

True to his word, Harrison had given Mackenzie all of the information he could find. She had it all by the time she was half an hour away from Salem. The information came in a mixture of texts and emails with attachments. And while there wasn't much to go on, Mackenzie thought she had more than enough.

She'd also taken some time during her drive to call ahead to the Salem Police Department. She asked if there would be anyone available to speak with her about the storage facility murders from five years ago. After a bit of shocked silence on the other end of the line, she was given the name of Detective Alan Hall.

With all of that information at the ready, Mackenzie started her trip to Salem with a visit to the police station. It appeared to be a run-of-the-mill slow day in the station. The receptionist was wiping down her desk with a cloth while three officers milled around a single desk in the back, chatting about something.

"Can I help you?" the receptionist asked.

"I'm Special Agent Mackenzie White. I'm supposed to meet with Detective Hall."

"Oh yes," the receptionist said. "Let me just get him up here for you."

The receptionist paged another office in the building through her phone and, after a few moments, said, "Your visitor is here."

"Thanks," Mackenzie said after she hung up.

"Sure. Where are you driving in from, if you don't mind my asking."

"Flew out of DC yesterday, to Seattle."

The receptionist tried to smile at this, but she was apparently adding things up in her head and deciding that something bad must have happened. Instead of trying to continue with chitchat, she turned back to cleaning her desk.

Before she had scrubbed a handful of times, a plainclothes detective came walking toward the little galley area where the receptionist was cleaning. He seemed a little surprised by the sight of Mackenzie but did his best to hide it. He was an older man, floating somewhere between fifty and fifty-five at Mackenzie's guess. He wore one of those little driver caps that some men look goofy in, but he pulled it off quite well.

"Agent White?" he asked.

"Pleased to meet you," she said, offering his hand when he stuck it out for a shake. "Nice to meet you, Detective Hall."

"You may change your mind about that soon enough," he said. "I'll level with you: this case haunts me. It damn near made me quit my job. So I'll help in any way I can, but I'd really rather not dwell on it."

"Of course," she said. "Do you mind if we speak in private somewhere?"

"How about in my car?" Hall said. "I'll tell you what I can on the way out to the first storage complex. It's about fifteen minutes away."

"That sounds good," she said.

Apparently, Hall wasn't one for formalities. He gave her a curt little nod and started heading for the front door without another word. Mackenzie followed him and started to feel some sort of odd dread creeping up on her.

This case haunts me, he had said.

Based on the look of unease in his eyes as he had turned toward the door, Mackenzie didn't doubt him one bit.

***

"He's doing it again, right?"

The question was out of Hall's mouth before they were even out of the parking lot. He had a look of certainty on his face, as if he had been expecting to hear such news for a very long time now.

"He is," she answered. "Or so it seems. In Seattle. What makes you sure enough to ask a question like that?"

"The way he went about killing them…just leaving them there to be found or rot…it doesn't make sense that he'd just stop. I think we got close to getting him, I really do. I think that's why he stopped when he did. But I've always felt that he'd pop up somewhere else and start again."

"We've got two bodies in Seattle so far," Mackenzie said. "One had been in the storage unit for quite some time. Seven to eight days at least."

Hall nodded. "A single stab wound to the gut?"

"Yes sir."

"I always thought he did that so they'd bleed out…die slow, you know? And that's what gets me about the case. The fourth body…she'd been there for at least three days. The coroner said she had just recently died. Like *very* recently. If we'd found her a few hours before…"

40

Hall looked through the windshield with a slate-solid look on his face. She'd seen that look on agents here and there—agents who had gone through some terrible traumatic case and had not quite fully recovered.

"The five cases out here," Mackenzie said. "I understand that there aren't many family members that stuck around?"

"That's one way of putting it. For one of the women, it was just too much for the family. Her brother committed suicide a week later and their father followed suit right after the funerals. The mother moved away somewhere else…last I heard it was somewhere overseas. She got as far away as possible. Two of them didn't have any family around here in the first place. As for the other two, I believe their families are still around Salem somewhere."

She let all of this sink in as Hall drove them through the light flow of traffic. Because she had left Seattle just before seven o'clock, it was not yet even noon when Hall pulled his car off of the highway and into a thin two-lane that emptied out into the parking lot of a place called Salem Storage.

She could tell right away that the place was no longer in business. The office building had wooden shutters over its single window and the gate that separated the storage sheds from the parking lot had been sloppily torn down. Hall parked in front of the derelict office and wasted no time in getting out.

"Went out of business about a year after the murders. Two of them occurred here."

"Do you know which ones?"

"Pamela Evans and Jade Barker."

She didn't doubt him when he pulled those names out so quickly. She imagined he knew every detail about the cases inside and out.

"Do you recall which one Jade Barker was discovered in?" she asked.

Hall nodded and started walking forward. He led her down the central aisle that ran between the storage buildings, keeping his eyes straight ahead. He didn't look spooked but very determined—determined not to let the past reach out and ensnare him. After about thirty seconds of walking, he stopped and pointed to one of the storage sheds on the right.

"That one."

Mackenzie walked up to it and was surprised to see that there was no lock. She wondered if the place had been more or less ransacked after the business and gone belly-up. She looked back to

Hall, as if making sure she was allowed to open it up. All he did was shrug as he stepped forward to join her.

He lifted the door for her. It shrieked on rusted gliders but folded in and up without too much of a problem. As Mackenzie had expected, the place was empty.

"Do you know if Jade Barker's family ended up getting her things?"

"I believe so. Her family is one of the ones that live nearby. Her parents took Jade's death incredibly hard. I bet you anything they still have most of her stuff from this little building. In his basement or attic or something."

Mackenzie stepped inside. It was very musty and moldy inside, thick with the scent of forgotten places and things. She found herself looking in the corners for trinkets left behind. But there was nothing, of course.

Nothing other than a faded stain near the front center. A stain that had once unmistakably been blood.

"You good here?" Hall asked. "There's one other thing I want to show you."

He turned and headed back for the car before Mackenzie had time to answer. He left her to look down at that stain and imagine the woman who had one lain there, gagged and bound and slowly bleeding out as she slowly started to starve.

A little shiver passed through Mackenzie. She tore her eyes away from the stained floor and quickly followed Hall out, left to close the door by herself.

***

Mackenzie sat in silence, thinking about the kind of person who would kill until nearly caught, then move somewhere else for safety only to start again eight years later. Why the huge span of time? Why go back to the exact same manner of killing?

He's a creature of habit, she thought. *That, plus the potential game of leaving bizarre tea party–themed clues behind will surely lead us to him…right?*

Hall drove them from Salem Storage to another storage site. Only, to call this one a storage complex was a stretch. It was an open lot three miles outside of the city limits, tucked away in the middle of a barren field. Mackenzie was confused as she stepped out of the car and followed Hall into the lot.

There were eight storage sheds sitting in the lot, all marked with graffiti of some kind or another. There were punctures in the side of one that she was pretty sure were bullet holes.

"The third victim, Shana Batiste, was found here. As you can see for yourself, this was just some little ramshackle operation run by a guy for extra cash. He was a truck driver who ran this on the side. Had his wife helping. The place was never much, as you can see. Just a quick way for some local shithead to make an extra grand or so a month."

He led them to one of the units at the far end of the lot. The door was already opened, hanging slightly crooked at the top like a chipped tooth. Hall nodded toward it, making it clear that he had no intention of going inside.

"We don't know for certain, but we think Shana Batiste might have been his first victim. When she was discovered, she'd been dead for at least three weeks. She was naked and had that cut in her upper stomach. There were bruises all along her back. She'd scratched at the door so much that her fingernails were chipped and bloody. When the coroner took the gag off of her mouth...her tongue..."

"It's okay," Mackenzie said, more for her own benefit than his. "You can stop."

Hall did so, gladly. He stood back while Mackenzie took a single step into the unit. Because of the opened door, the inside was littered with old moldy leaves, little scant piles of dust and dirt, and rat droppings. Still, it just had the feel of a place where a lot of vile things had gone down; it was a feeling she was starting to trust, some sort of weird sensor in her heart or brain that was becoming finely tuned as her career went on.

"Is her family still around?" Mackenzie asked.

"Just a grandmother. And she's in an assisted living home about an hour away with dementia."

There was nothing worthwhile in the unit, but that was okay with Mackenzie. If Hall had needed to bring her out here to show her just what he'd had to endure, she could forgive him for that.

"I got a partial inventory list from two of the sites," Mackenzie said. "You were present at all five sites, correct?"

"That's right."

"Was there anything at all that stuck out to you?" she asked. "Anything that seemed out of place or sitting outside of all of the boxes and bins that just looked randomly placed?"

He looked her in the eyes, his stare locked and cold. "Why do you ask?"

43

"I'm working a hunch…some things I've seen at the two sites in Seattle. It seems like a weak link—even almost coincidental. But if I could tie it back to the murders here…"

"Little tea cups," Hall said. "In two of the units. And then right here in Shana Batiste's unit, there were these cutesy little play food things—pretend grapes, bread, butter. Like a kid plays with, you know?"

"Yeah, I know…"

And that was all that needed to be said by either of them. Everything else was communicated in their eyes—that this was a definite link. And that it made the murders much more disturbing.

"Shit," Hall said.

And with that, he lowered his head and went back to the car. Mackenzie stood there a moment longer, looking back into the decrepit unit as if trying to peer into its bloody past.

CHAPTER TWELVE

Back at the station, Hall invited her in for coffee. It was inching in near one o'clock in the afternoon and Mackenzie wanted to be back on the road no later than four, but she accepted. She thought it might be borderline cruel to make Detective Hall relive the hell he'd lived through eight years ago and then just leave him to his thoughts.

As she sat down in his office and he handed her a cup from the Keurig in the corner of the room, it was as if he read her thoughts. He sat down and let out a deep sigh.

"I imagine you want to get back to Seattle as quickly as possible," he said. "While you were hanging back at the last unit, I called ahead and had one of the officers get together the information on any family members of the victims that are still around here. As it turns out, I was wrong. There's only one family close by. The second closest is about two and a half hours away, out near the coast somewhere."

"Which family is still in Salem?"

"The Barkers. Jade Barker's parents are both still living in Salem. The father was hospitalized for a while after Jade's death. He wasn't eating well, got dehydrated, and just fell flat out sick. Jade had a brother, too. But he's serving some time in prison for attempted rape and damn near beating some guy to death outside of a bar—both events occurring the weekend after his sister's funeral. Needless to say, those five bodies found so close together with no hope of finding the killer…it tore these families apart."

Mackenzie sipped from her coffee as Detective Hall slid a piece of paper over to her. It was a plain sheet of notebook paper, with an address.

"Debbie Barker is newly retired and sells some sort of upcycled crafts at local farmer's markets," Hall said. "Chances are pretty good you'll catch her at home."

Mackenzie took the slip of paper and downed more of her coffee. "I know this wasn't easy for you, Detective. Thank you for your help."

"No problem. Just…do me a favor and catch this guy, would you?"

She smiled a little nervously. "I intend to. And you'll be among the first to know when I do."

***

Just before she pulled into the driveway of the Barker residence, Mackenzie wondered how Detective Hall had known so much about the Barkers. She assumed it was because he had kept tabs on them after the murder of their daughter. It was something that police officers and agents sometimes fell into when they were unable to solve a case. They cast all of their feelings of failures and inadequacy into making sure they knew how the relatives were doing, how they were holding up. It was a noble thing, but also quite sad as well.

As it turned out, Hall had been absolutely correct in his assumption. When Mackenzie got out of her car in the Barkers' driveway at 1:45, she saw the garage door open and could hear the whirring of some small electrical appliance. As she walked up the driveway and got closer to the garage, she was able to see inside. She saw a woman of about sixty or so hunched over a work bench with a small hand-sander. She was working on an oval-shaped object, oblivious to the rest of the world.

Mackenzie waited a moment, not wanting to scare her. She did not make her presence known until the woman—presumably Debbie Barker—shut the sander down and removed the protective eyewear from her head. Mackenzie knocked lightly on the edge of the garage and said, "Hello."

Debbie turned around with a bit of a jump and smiled uncertainly. "Um, hello. Can I help you?" There was sawdust in her hair and on her shirt and, despite her unexpected visitor, she looked rather happy. Mackenzie hated where she was about to take this woman.

"Yes, you can," she said. "I'm Special Agent Mackenzie White, with the FBI. I know it might seem sudden and out of the blue, but I was wondering if I could ask you some questions about your daughter."

The slight smile on Debbie Barker's face faded. She shook her head and turned immediately back to her project, already picking the sander back up. "No thanks," she said. "That part of my life is behind me and as you know, Jade is no longer with us."

"With all due respect, there were four others as well," Mackenzie said. "And now there are two more."

Debbie hesitated. She didn't turn back around to face Mackenzie. She just stood there as if frozen in place. "When?" she asked.

46

"Just within the last week or so. In Seattle. The sites and the way it's happening are seemingly identical to what happened here in Salem. I'd like to think we can bring this guy in this time but I need your help."

Debbie finally turned back around. She was crying, the sander and her project now forgotten. "You have to understand how painful it is for me to go back to that time," she said. "It destroyed not just our family but…it ruined everything. It took years to move on."

"And that's why I'll keep the questions low-key and as non-intrusive as I can. Does that sound okay?"

"What do you need to know? I talked to what seemed like hundreds of policemen and FBI agents. I don't have anything new to offer."

"Well, I was curious about the sort of things Jade kept in her unit. You ended up with a great deal of her things, right?"

"I did. It's all up in the attic but—and please don't take this the wrong way—I'm not about to let you tear through it."

"I wouldn't expect you to," Mackenzie said. "But what I'm interested in learning about is if there was anything in the unit that you didn't expect. Was there anything out of the ordinary?"

Debbie let out a laugh and looked down at her hands, as if there was a joke written there. "Yeah, some things did shock me. She was apparently a fan of those trashy period romance novels with the guy with his shirt ripped off on the front. She always told me she preferred classic stuff, you know? But…yikes. Those terrible novels. You know the kind?"

"I do. Anything else?"

"Yes," Debbie said curtly. It almost seemed as if she didn't want to keep going. "There was a pitcher and a little plate. But they were toys, you know? Like tea party stuff. At the time, right after we found her, I didn't even think twice about it. But as I moved her stuff here, me and her father, I saw those things. They were unpacked and just sort of sitting there by themselves. And it made no sense for Jade to have them. All this time I figured it might have been some inside joke between her and her old roommate in college. But I asked her roommate about it a few years back and she said she had no idea."

"It might sound odd," Mackenzie said, "but do you think you'd be willing to part with them?"

Debbie considered it for a moment and then nodded. "I guess so. It's done nothing but raise questions anyway. Do you think they're related to the cases in some way?"

47

The truth was, Mackenzie was pretty certain they *were* related. But telling Debbie Barker that would do nothing but raise painful memories. "We don't know yet," she said. "We're just doing everything we can to ensure that the Seattle cases are indeed linked to the Salem cases. And for now, we're pursuing every avenue we can."

The look on Debbie's face made it clear that she knew she was being fed a line of bullshit. Still, she nodded and headed for the door that led inside. "Give me a second," she said as she entered the door, making it quite clear that Mackenzie was not allowed inside.

While she waited, Mackenzie pulled out her phone and texted Ellington. **Any luck on your end?**

She pocketed the phone and looked around at the things Debbie was creating. From what Mackenzie could tell, Debbie was making high-end farmhouse objects. There was a sign with a stenciled coffee cup on it, and another that said MENU with a perfect little square for a chalkboard to go into.

While she looked, her phone dinged. It was a return text from Ellington. **Slow but productive. Family members of the victims have all but been ruled out. Most of the questioning done. You?**

She quickly responded with: **Things have been eye-opening here in Oregon.**

In the same moment she pocketed the phone, the door into the house opened. Debbie Barker stepped out, holding a small plastic bag. She handed it over to Mackenzie as if there were rotting food inside of it.

"I hope it helps," Debbie said. "And I hope you can find the monster that did this. I just can't even imagine the sort of person who would…"

Mackenzie wouldn't even allow herself to nod. She knew where Debbie was going with the comment, of course, but she had seen more than enough people in her career who *were* capable of such a thing.

She'd also seen the family members of victims, years removed from the trauma. After a while, they tended to no longer think of the person who took the lives of their loved ones as a mere human; in their minds, the killer became a boogeyman or a monster.

But Mackenzie knew that this was not the case. She knew that there were no monsters, only monstrous drives in the hearts of men. And because of that—because she was only after men and not monsters—she knew she had a good chance at catching them.

As she stood in Debbie's garage, a broken mother who had worked hard to put the past behind her, Mackenzie vowed to herself that the man who had taken the life of Debbie Barker's daughter would be no different.

CHAPTER THIRTEEN

Kelly Higdon knew she wasn't going to make it back to work on time, but she didn't care. It was one of those days where she had a million things to do over the course of her hour-long lunch break. Besides…no one ever came back when they were supposed to. She worked at the kind of place where some people came back from lunch with margaritas on their breath or, as was the case with her supervisor and the married receptionist, reeking of sex.

So if she was yelled at for being fifteen minutes late for trying to cram four errands into the space of an hour, they could kiss her ass. She hated the job anyway. She wanted to be a journalist, not writing dry and often bloated proposals for a telecom company.

She came to the destination of her final errand with that mindset driving her. She drove through the main gate of Griffin Brothers Storage City, listening to the contents of the cardboard box in her backseat rattling around. Everything in that box had been in her boyfriend's apartment forty minutes ago. When he came home and found them missing, maybe he'd figure out that she was dumping him without calling for an explanation. And if he did call, then she'd send him the picture she had been texted earlier in the day. A picture of her boyfriend's unmentionables in another woman's mouth—a picture that had been taken as some sort of foreplay or turn-on game by the woman in the picture.

Kelly drove through the wide alley that sat between the rows of units. It was 12:50 in the afternoon so there was practically no one there. Therefore, she didn't bother parking all nice and perfect in front of her unit. Besides, she was just going to drop the box off and leave.

She got out of the car, grabbed the box out of the back, and punched in the five-digit code on her lock. She heard the click, grabbed the handle, and gave it a hefty push up. It opened to reveal her rather messy storage unit. She knew she needed to clean it out eventually; she had shit from childhood that she knew she didn't need or even want. She was a pack rat, plain and simple. As she set her box down among the stacks of her belongings, she spotted her old Strawberry Shortcake record player.

Seriously, Kelly, she thought. *What in the hell do you need that for?*

This thought was interrupted by a voice from behind her.

"Hey, um, could you move your car?"

She turned around, trying to hide the irritation from her face. She saw a man standing there, looking quite embarrassed to even be asking the question at all.

"Sorry," she said. "I was just leaving."

He turned to leave her alone, giving a quick nod of thanks. As she started out too, she noticed that he had stopped at her car. He took a quick look around and then turned back to her.

The blow seemed to come out of nowhere. She was too busy trying to figure out what he was holding in his hand to think about warding off the hit. She heard and felt the blow when it came and as she stumbled to the ground, she finally saw the length of steel pipe in his hand in a hazy sort of blur.

He came into the unit with her then and she tried to get a look at his face but the world went dark before she could focus on those maniacal black eyes.

***

When Kelly opened her eyes again, she thought she was going to throw up. The pain in her head was monstrous. She tried to cry out but discovered that her mouth was taped shut. Below her, the world seemed to be moving. She was being jostled around, which she assumed was why she had managed to come to.

She then recalled being struck by the lead pipe and the man coming into her storage unit.

Kelly squealed beneath the tape and the noise was weak, like the sound of a creaky door. In response, she felt something squeeze tight around her back. She moaned against the tape and then did her best to settle herself, to figure out just what the hell was happening to her.

She didn't have time for this, though. As soon as she decided to try to calm herself, she felt herself falling. It was a very short fall. She landed on something relatively soft and then, for the moment, she was stationary. She took that moment to look up and take inventory of the situation.

She was in a small room. There were a few boxes located around the room, pushed up against the wall. A single bulb shone down on her from a roof that looked to be made of tin or some sort of metal.

A storage unit…but not mine. Where the hell…?

A man stepped into her view. She recognized him at once. He was not holding a lead pipe this time, but that made him no less

51

sinister. Kelly tried to crawl away but could not. Her hands were bound behind her and when she tried to back up, it put incredible strain on her shoulders. She also found that her feet were bound in the same way, with rope or some kind of cord.

"I know you're scared," the man said. "But it will be over before you know it. From what I understand, when you start to lose enough blood, time goes by very fast as your brain starts to panic…as your heart starts to slow down."

Kelly wanted to beg for her life, wanted to tell him she'd do anything he wanted if he'd let her go.

But the gag would not let her speak. And besides that, the look he had in his eyes told her that he was beyond bargaining. He already had what he wanted.

Kelly started to cry. The tears came quick, blurring her vision.

It was a slight mercy, really. The tears clouded her vision and she did not see the knife when he slowly descended on her.

CHAPTER FOURTEEN

Mackenzie returned to Seattle at 6:12 that evening. It was drizzling rain yet again but it did not bother her as much as it had the day before. As she walked into the police department with the bag Debbie Barker had given her, she felt like they finally had a path to follow. Of course, they had no idea how to truly travel down that path, but at least it gave them a clear avenue to pursue.

She found Ellington in the tiny conference room they were working out of. He was standing in front of a dry erase board where he had pinned a geographical map of the area and penned the names of the storage facilities. At the small table, Deputy Rising and another policeman sat with papers and files scattered around the table.

It was awkward to have them there. Mackenzie's first reaction to seeing her fiancé at work was to kiss him. Of course, that would not be appropriate, so she simply joined Rising and the other officer at the table.

"You bring us dinner?" Ellington asked, pointing to the plastic bag she carried in.

"No. What I'm bringing us is a clear link between the Salem, Oregon, cases and our two murders."

She then filled them in on her conversation with Debbie Barker and the time she had spent with Detective Hall. As she went through it all, she set the play pitcher and plate on the table. As she did, Rising slid two pictures on the table as well. Someone had apparently recently taken pictures of the little teapot and the doll that had been found at the Newcomb and Locke murder scenes.

"I'll admit," Rising said, "I thought trying to follow a trail based on a doll and a teapot was a little farfetched. But this sort of seals it for me."

"Yeah, she's pretty good like that," Ellington said with a wink toward Mackenzie. "Any thoughts on what we're going for here, Agent White?"

"Teapots and plates and dolls suggests to me that the killer has some weird tea party theme in mind. Why? I have no idea. And why leave them so easily out in sight? He wants us to see these things, but why?"

"Living out some messed up childhood fantasy?" Rising suggested.

"No clue," Mackenzie said. "But I think we have to at least consider that possibility. Plus, as strange as the connections may seem, we now know two things about him. He likes to store his victims in their own storage units, and he has a thing for tea party–related items."

"Meanwhile," Ellington said, "we've been trying to figure out a pattern to where he might strike next. There are twenty-one storage unit complexes in the city and another twelve in surrounding smaller towns. Sadly, two existing sites just aren't enough to triangulate on anything. We can't predict anything yet."

"Any idea why he's choosing storage sheds at all?" Rising asked.

"No, but it's a great question," Mackenzie said. "It could be because they feel so isolated and confined."

"They?" Ellington asked. "You mean the storage units or the killer?"

She'd meant the units but the way Ellington phrased the question made her wonder. Surely if a killer was sticking to small spaces to store his dead and then leaving playful keepsakes at the scenes, there had to be a psychological aspect to why he was doing these things.

"Did you get any feeling as to why the killer wrapped things up in Oregon?" Rising asked.

"Well, it's a much smaller area in Salem. Eventually, the net would have grown too tight as he ran out of storage complexes to use."

"And he still racked up five bodies," Ellington said. "With a city the size of Seattle, there's no telling how much he can get done."

"So what the hell do we do?" Rising asked.

"How much manpower can you give us?" Mackenzie asked.

"As much as you need."

"Good. I think it might be unrealistic to keep an eye on every storage facility in the area. But I do think every owner should be notified. They need to know to take extra security precautions. They need to know what's going on, but without spooking their clientele. But for now, I'd like to revisit something Agent Ellington asked…about if I was referring to the storage units as isolated and confined or the killer. What if the killer feels that way? What if it's an aspect of his personality that he's reflecting in the murders?"

"That's deep shit," Rising said.

"It is. Do you guys have a psychologist on staff here?"

"No," Rising said. "But we do all see the same shrink. An older lady that specializes in working with law enforcement and soldiers with PTSD."

"Would you be willing to call her as soon as possible to see if she'd speak with me? If she can do it in the next few hours, that would be ideal."

"Sure thing," Rising said. He waved to the other officer to follow him. They left the room quickly, leaving Ellington and Mackenzie to themselves.

Mackenzie surprised herself when she practically marched across the room and kissed Ellington. It was no innocent little *hello, how are you* sort of kiss, either. It was a passionate one that spoke volumes. He returned it, if not a little hesitantly, and when she felt his hands at her back, she felt herself relaxing.

Ellington broke the kiss after about five seconds. He looked at her, amused and curious. "What was that?"

"I don't know," she said. "Just...some of the stories I heard today in Salem were rough. And then I got in here and saw you hard at work...I just needed to kiss you. Is that okay?"

"That is absolutely okay," he said. "Are *you* okay?"

"I'll be better when we can summon up a tangible lead in this case. I hate to sound defeatist, but I'm not getting a good feeling about this one."

"Yeah, it's not looking promising, is it? I hate these cases where you almost have to have someone come up dead in the hopes of getting more clues."

The weight of that remark hung between them. She kissed him once more, this one nothing more than a peck on the cheek, and sat back down. She stared at the little plate and teapot as if willing them to offer up answers from their pasts.

CHAPTER FIFTEEN

Having heard about the two recent murders, the police psychologist had seemed pleased to meet with Mackenzie and Ellington. She volunteered to meet with them over a late dinner around eight o'clock, which had Mackenzie and Ellington rushing back to their hotel. Mackenzie loved to travel but the one thing she did not like about it was the stagnant feeling she sometimes felt on her afterward.

While Ellington checked his email and fielded a call from Deputy Rising, Mackenzie hopped in the shower. As she washed, she could not get the haunted look in Detective Hall's eyes out of her mind. She also clearly saw the interior of that last ramshackle storage unit gone to waste and something about it chilled her.

She thought of a killer checking out the sites of his abductions, already planning to take them elsewhere as a final resting place. That meant he was having to travel with them, to haul them from one place to the other. And based on forensic results, they were all betting on the victims being alive when they were dumped.

Unless he's waiting on them at the units and then attacking them there, she thought.

It was a good theory, but the video evidence from the Claire Locke murder did not support it. For someone to have gone to the complex and waited for her and then left, that meant the footage would have shown the same car coming and going, as well as showing Claire Locke arriving but not leaving afterward. And there was no such occurrence on that footage.

Her thoughts were interrupted by the sound of the shower curtain sliding open. Startled, she turned and saw Ellington. He was peering in at her, just as naked as she was.

"You clean yet?" he asked.

"Yeah, almost done."

"Oh," he said, disappointed. He started to close the curtain back but Mackenzie stopped him.

"It's a shower," she said, pulling him in. "It won't take much to get clean again."

Smiling, he joined her and they picked up where they'd left off in the conference room.

***

The psychologist's name was Janell Harper. She was sixty-one but looked fifty and when Mackenzie and Ellington met her at the restaurant of her choice for dinner, she was enjoying a glass of red wine while reading something on her phone. She looked up at Mackenzie and Ellington as they sat down and Mackenzie decided at once that she liked her. Harper did not bother with a fake smile or pleasantries. She knew why they were here and didn't bother pretending that everything was fine.

"Thanks for meeting with us," Mackenzie said. "I know it was very last minute."

"Not a problem at all. I'd heard about the one murder…but this second one was news to me. Are you suspecting a serial killer?"

"We know it's a serial," Mackenzie said. "He's done this before, in Oregon. Five victims and he was never caught."

"My God," Harper said.

"It was the same in Oregon," Ellington said. "Bodies stored in storage units in an injured and bound state. They were left there to starve or bleed out—whichever came first."

"What can you tell me about the killer?" Harper asked.

"Well, that's why we came to you," Mackenzie said. "He leaves his crime scenes clean. No prints, no hairs, nothing. He stabs them once in the upper stomach, the cut almost always in the exact same place. And then he leaves them."

"Any signs of rape or molestation?" Harper asked.

"All signs point to no, but the pathologist hasn't one hundred percent ruled it out."

"He will, I suspect," Harper said. "If there was sex involved, it would be evident. Anyone who binds and gags someone—it's about control and dominance. So if he was having sex with the women, he'd humiliate and dominate them in that way as well."

"He *does* seem to be leaving behind little puzzle pieces," Mackenzie said. "A doll in one unit. A play teapot in another. Toy plates and pitchers in others."

"That makes me think he's either mourning or celebrating something from his childhood. He's trying to get a tea party together. While the act may seem morbid to us, we have to peek into the mindset of someone who has no problem capturing, binding, and killing women. This tea party he seems to want to set up may be the key. Of course, it's just symbolic. But he may not know this."

She stopped here, as the waiter came by the table and took their orders. Mackenzie realized that she was ravenous and ordered a surf and turf dinner. And she was already considering what she might have for dessert. With their orders placed, the waiter left them alone again. Mackenzie picked up exactly where they had left off.

"When you think of the storage units as the location for the end game of each murder, what do you see in terms of personality?" Mackenzie asked.

"Well, it's very interesting because it could go one of two ways. My first instinct is that he has a hoarding mentality—that the concept of keeping things stored in safe places where they are easily accessible appeals to him. But even that in and of itself is contradictory because as a general rule, hoarders aren't much for organization."

"So you think he enjoys the idea of keeping his victims in a place where he can easily find them later?" Ellington asked.

"Perhaps. But I feel that my first instinct might be closest to the truth. If he's leaving these women unattended in storage units, it might be because he fears them getting lost elsewhere. And when you tie the tea party paraphernalia into it as well, I think it points back to where he grew up. I'd bet you the bill for our dinner that the killer grew up in a house that was very messy and cluttered."

"That makes sense, but it doesn't really help us profile the killer."

"Sure it does. A bit, anyway. Your killer is likely not a very messy person. It might be why he only stabs them once and leaves. It also suggests that he might be storing them in these units because he doesn't want their bodies to make a mess anywhere. His house, his car, even the victims' homes."

"It would also explain why he's not leaving any physical traces behind at the crime scenes," Ellington said.

"Tell me…of the storage units you've seen him use, were they tidy or just crammed full of stuff stacked haphazardly to the walls?"

"There were one or two that I wouldn't have considered immaculate," Mackenzie said. "But for the most part, yes…they've been well organized and tidied up."

"It makes me wonder if they were like that *before* the killer used them," Harper said.

"You think he's cleaning the place after he stabs them?" Ellington asked.

"I think it's a possibility. I have a storage unit myself. So does my mother-in-law. Neither of them would be considered clean. I know where everything is, but it's still nothing more than a vaguely organized chaos. I won't make such a brash assumption and say that *all* storage units are like that, but I would venture a guess to say that more are disorganized than not."

It certainly gave Mackenzie something to think about. She wasn't sure if it helped to develop a profile on the killer or not, but it did open up a whole new perspective on the case.

"There's another thing I wonder if you've considered," Harper said. "Profiling aside, the killer might very well be using the storage units because of how infrequently they are used. I hate to put the idea in your head if it isn't already there, but what if there are more out there? Many more? And it's just a matter of someone finding them?"

"Cold cases," Mackenzie said, feeling absolutely inferior in the moment. "Missing persons reports."

"Shit," Ellington said.

It wasn't exactly an avenue they had missed, but one that had been staring them in the face and had simply not yet been noticed.

"Please know," Harper said, "that I don't offer that suggestion under the assumption that you're not doing your job well. But if we're going with the line of thought that this killer had some sort of aversion to messiness or even clutter, he'd opt for locations that would go undisturbed for quite some time. Sure, he could dump them in the woods, but the woods in and of themselves are quite messy."

"And I guess it's harder to have a tea party out in the dark woods," Ellington said in a joking tone.

"You jest, but there's something to that. This killer wants things clean. Organized. Undisturbed. But the tea party aspect insinuates that there's something more to it. Something he maybe missed out on as a child as a result of a messy home or a lack of organization."

Mackenzie's mind was reeling, trying to connect trains of thought so they'd all run on the same track. Nothing Janell Harper had given them were huge revelations by any stretch of the imagination, but it *did* give Mackenzie many new angles to view the case from.

Their dinner arrived, and Mackenzie ate as quickly as she could without seeming too unladylike. The conversation did not stall, but they only discussed the two Seattle murders in more detail. Every new detail they gave Harper only had her nodding, reinforcing her sketched-out profile.

Mackenzie was already thinking of cold cases and missing persons reports. She knew that even one missing persons report or abduction account could very well lead them to the killer.

Unfortunately, in a city the size of Seattle, finding one case to connect to their killer would not be easy. But they had to start somewhere.

With this plan hatching in her head, Mackenzie slowed her eating a bit. She decided to enjoy it…because she had a long night of digging ahead of her.

CHAPTER SIXTEEN

Mackenzie and Ellington headed back to the police station directly after their dinner with Janell Harper. While Mackenzie connected her laptop to the department's network, Ellington called up Deputy Rising to see if he wanted to lend a hand. Within half an hour, they had a little information center set up in the small conference room. Rising had enlisted the help of two other officers, a female officer named Dentry and an aging man named Willard.

As the first hour passed, Mackenzie had the printer humming, printing out case files and reports. She also had the whiteboard mostly covered in notes. She and Ellington were working on collecting cold cases within a thirty-mile range over the past eight years while Dentry and Willard looked over any missing persons cases within the past year. They identified seven possible cases that fit the description—women between the ages of eighteen and fifty—and started to dig into them.

Meanwhile, Rising was looking deeper into the rental process for the storage unit complexes that Claire Locke and Elizabeth Newcomb had been discovered in. The hope was that they could perhaps find some clues, no matter how small. How long had they been renting the unit? Did they pay on time? Had either of the women complained about possible break-ins to their units?

It wasn't the most glamorous way to crack a case, but Mackenzie had always appreciated the old-fashioned art of sitting down and just drowning in research. Sometimes it wasn't a high-speed chase or last-minute thrill that cracked a case; sometimes it was simple research.

At 9:55, Officer Dentry brought a two-page file to Mackenzie. She looked a little relieved, as if she was holding in excitement. For a moment, Mackenzie wondered if the woman had managed to find the clue that was going to help them find the killer.

"This file is on a woman named Angela Hernandez," Dentry said. "She was reported missing eight months ago by her husband. Of the seven active cases we came across, she most closely resembles what we're looking for. She rented a storage unit over at U-Store-It."

"Do we know if any family members cleaned it out after her disappearance?" Mackenzie asked.

"No way of knowing," Dentry said.

"Get a man named Ralph Underwood on the phone. He's the owner of U-Store-It. Tell him that Agents White and Ellington need to know everything there is to know about the unit belonging to Angela Hernandez."

Dentry nodded and as she left the room, another thought occurred to Mackenzie. As odd as it seemed, speaking with Janell Harper had unlocked some mental door. She was now allowing herself to explore the case from all angles and it was unearthing new ideas.

She took out her phone and dialed up a number she had been given earlier in the day. It rang three times before Detective Alan Hall answered. "Hello?"

"Detective Hall, I'm sorry to bother you at such an hour, but I was wondering if you might be able to lend me some information on the storage unit cases. Something I overlooked earlier today."

"If I know the answers, sure, I'd like to help however I can."

"I'd like to see if I can find out how long each unit had been rented by the victims before their deaths. I'd also like to know if they were rented in cash or with a credit card. Lastly, I'd like to know the names that they were rented under. Consider it a red flag if it was anyone's name other than the victim's."

"Should be easy to get you that stuff. I'm pretty sure it's all in the last case file that was put together. I'm at home, though. Let me call the station and get someone to email it to me. Give me half an hour or so?"

"Sooner would be better, but I'll take an hour. Thanks."

She ended the call and looked to the dry erase board, covered in her notes. Quietly, Ellington sat down next to her. "What are you thinking?" he asked.

"Nothing yet."

"Liar. I know that look. You're rummaging around in that head of yours. You think you're on to something, don't you?"

"Maybe. But we need to see what information Dentry and Detective Hall come back to us with."

"You have to fill me in somehow," he said.

"It's a stretch, but I'm wondering how preplanned all of these murders were. They had to be followed extensively. Almost *too* extensively. It almost makes no sense. The killer had to know where the units were beforehand so he could be there waiting for them. And that makes me think he had a unit in the same places. Or…"

"Or what?"

Mackenzie wasn't sure how to finish her thought. As it turned out, she didn't have the opportunity to do so. Dentry came back in the room with an annoyed look on her face. She was holding her cell phone out to Mackenzie, shaking her head.

"He says he wants to talk to you."

"Ralph Underwood?"

Dentry nodded. "I think he might have what you're looking for but he's…well, he's sort of an asshole."

Mackenzie took the phone and wasted no time. "Mr. Underwood, I assure you that the local police are more than capable of fielding your information."

"Maybe. But I don't need local noses in my business once you and your other bureau friends are out of town."

Deciding to skip past a possible empty argument, Mackenzie settled straight to the point. "Mr. Underwood, what is it you wanted to tell me?"

"Well, the other woman was asking about the Newcomb unit. I'm here at home and have all of my records on my laptop. I have all the answers she wanted but wanted to give them to you myself."

"Fine. Thank you," she said, irritated with him but also trying to pacify their one source of reliable information.

"Elizabeth Newcomb had been renting this unit for eighteen months. She always paid on time and she always paid with cash. But here's the interesting part—and I feel stupid for not just remembering it."

"What's that?" Mackenzie asked, hoping for a break.

"When she rented it, she did it in someone else's name. It's not her name on the application, but she's the one that always used it and paid for it."

"What name is on the application then?"

"Mark Riley. And the address is right here in Seattle."

"That's perfect, Mr. Underwood. Thank y—"

"But there's something else, too. That's not the only unit I have here under the name of Mark Riley. He has two more."

"And he pays regularly?"

"Yes."

"Do you have any way of tracking who visits the units at any given time?" she asked.

"No. There's no sign-in or check-in."

"That's fine," Mackenzie said. "Mr. Underwood, would you allow us to visit your complex again later tonight and take a look at those units?"

"That's fine. Do you need me there?"

"It might come in handy. Why don't you meet us there in about an hour?"

As he answered in the positive, Mackenzie got a beep. She checked the display and saw that it was the Salem, Oregon, area code. It was Detective Hall, already calling back.

"Mr. Underwood, we'll see you in about an hour. I have to grab this call waiting now. But thanks for your help."

She switched lines, feeling that they really were starting to make progress now. "Detective Hall, thanks for getting back in touch with me."

"Of course. Now, I'm looking at this final report and everything checks out…everything except one small detail. There was one unit that was checked out under a different name than the woman who was renting it."

"Do you have the name?"

"I do. Does the name Mark Riley mean anything to you?"

CHAPTER SEVENTEEN

After calling Ralph Underwood back, Mackenzie was able to get the address for a Mark Riley in Seattle. The address, of course, was very different from the one Detective Hall had provided. A quick check of the Salem, Oregon, address revealed that the address had not been viable for more than two years. It was, in fact, an apartment in a building that had been condemned last year.

"You think we'll find another abandoned place when we follow this up?" Deputy Rising asked Mackenzie as he headed out of the station with her and Ellington.

"I don't know. Probably. This guy covers his tracks pretty damn good. It seems strange that he'd overlook something as stupid as freely giving his name in two different locations."

"We'll know who Mark Riley is within fifteen minutes," Rising said. "Dentry and Willard are running the name right now."

With the feeling of some sort of progress finally pushing them along, Mackenzie, Ellington, and Rising rolled out of the lot, Rising leading the way to the address Ralph Underwood had on file for Mark Riley.

In their car, following behind Rising, Ellington let out a sigh. "Something about this doesn't seem right. I feel like we might be rolling into a trap."

"I thought so, too," Mackenzie said. "But if this is some kind of set-up for us, I don't think it's going to be anything dangerous. These clues this jackass is leaving behind…it makes me think he wants us to figure it out. He's trying to tell us something…something that the agents back in Salem eight years ago weren't able to decipher."

"Still…feels like a wild goose chase. Feels like he's just dragging us along."

"Well, you know, the alternative could be true," Mackenzie pointed out. "He could have just screwed up, thinking we wouldn't catch on to him. Maybe he thought the fact that he had paid cash would keep him off the radar."

"You know, there's also the fact that Elizabeth Newcomb might very well have known this guy since his name was on the lease."

"That *does* raise a lot of questions," Mackenzie said. "But hopefully all of that will be answered shortly."

Ahead of them, Rising was going about fifteen miles over the speed limit. He had elected not to run his flashers, instead going for the element of surprise—a good choice, seeing as how he was leading them to the outskirts of the city. They'd been on the road for about twenty minutes when he turned off of a generic two-lane and onto a little stretch of road that led into a rundown urban district.

The houses along this street were simple one-story domiciles, the porches thick with clutter, the yards mostly dead and gray. Rising led them down two blocks of this neighborhood before pulling his car alongside the curb. Mackenzie parked behind him, taking in a good view of the surrounding yards before she killed the headlights.

She hated to ever fall into stereotypes, but this was the type of neighborhood that just made her think of drug deals and inner-city gangs. Yet as she and Ellington stepped out of the car, the streets were silent. Somewhere very far away they could hear the muffled sound of an engine revving up, but there was nothing else.

They joined Rising in front of the house he had parked alongside. Ellington took the lead, walking up the cracked sidewalk. Even before they reached the porch, Mackenzie was fairly certain the place was deserted. Not that there was simply no one home, but that there was no one living there at all—maybe not for a few years. It just had that look to it, from the partially collapsed porch banisters to the cracked window on the left side of the porch. An overturned lawn chair sitting in the corner of the porch alongside broken beer bottles was the last giveaway.

"Told you," Ellington said as he stepped up onto the porch. "We've been played. Not a fake address, but one that might as well be."

"But why?" Rising asked.

"To screw with us," Ellington said. "To make him feel smarter than we are."

The trio stood in the darkness for a moment, considering. Mackenzie then walked up the steps and looked at the door. She withdrew her little Maglite and ran the small light beam over the door frame.

The frame was still intact. She gave the door a hefty push but it did not budge. She looked to Ellington with a wicked little smile. "Would you?"

"I don't see the point," he said. "He's just messing with us."

She gave him a scowl and then shrugged. She took two steps backward, getting into a posture that would allow her to deliver a

66

solid kick to the door. She looked back to Ellington one more time, giving him a playful look that she used quite a bit to give him last chances to change his mind. It worked most of the time, from trying to decide what to watch on TV to what they would have for dinner. Sure, the environment was different now, but the look still worked.

"Ah, hell," Ellington said. "Move aside."

She smiled. She was fully capable of kicking the door down but she knew Ellington liked to take the lead on things like this. Sometimes it just took some pushing.

Ellington reared back and delivered a vicious kick, his foot landing squarely beside the knob and lock. The door shuddered and didn't so much fly open as it caved in. It shattered into several pieces as one of the hinges popped off.

Yeah, this house hasn't been lived in in quite some time, Mackenzie thought.

Ellington and Rising now took out their own flashlights as they walked into the house. The place had been completely cleared out, no furniture, no pictures on the wall, nothing. There were cobwebs everywhere, and rat droppings scattered here and there. The wood floor had a large discolored patch covering most of it, indicating that it had once been covered in carpet. A tangle of old cords extended from the wall where a TV stand once sat.

"Yeah, I think this was a wild goose chase," Rising said. He was standing in the large entryway between the kitchen and the living room. Mackenzie could see that in the kitchen, the stove had even been removed.

She wasn't ready to admit that this was a waste of time just yet. She entered the hallway that extended off of the right side of the living room. Like the rest of the house, the hallway was short and neglected. A chunk of plaster had been torn from the wall to her right. A single door on that side of the hallway led into a small bathroom. There was dirt and grime in the sink and a brown stain in the bathtub.

There was only one other room along the hall. It was at the end of the hall, the door opened wide to reveal the darkness beyond. Mackenzie couldn't help the flush of fear that ran through her, the primal fear of the unknown ahead of her. She shone the Maglite inside as she approached the doorway, seeing the glow of beams from Ellington and Rising behind her.

She stepped through the doorway and found a mostly empty room. There was no furniture, just like the rest of the house. There were marks and dings in the wall. A broken light fixture hung haphazardly from the ceiling.

But in the middle of the floor directly in front of her, a doll had been propped up against an old phone book. It looked up at her with dead, glassy eyes.

Mackenzie was almost ashamed at how frightened she was in that moment.

"Mac?"

Ellington stepped up beside her, his flashlight beam joining hers. The doll was fully illuminated now. More than that, the scrap of paper sitting in the fork of its little legs was hard to miss with all the light on it.

"Find something?" Rising asked as he joined them. When he saw the doll, he let out a quiet little curse under his breath.

Mackenzie slowly stepped toward the doll. She bent down and picked up the scrap of paper. It was a plain sheet of notebook paper that had been torn in half and then folded. It did not look like a fresh piece, but it was certainly much newer than the dust piles adrift in the house.

Behind her, Rising's cell phone rang. The noise caused all three of them to jump. Mackenzie thought she saw Rising even going for his sidearm. They all breathed a sigh of relief, overlooking their embarrassment at being so easily spooked. Rising answered it with a look of irritation.

"Yeah?" he asked.

Mackenzie slowly unfolded the paper as they listened to Rising's conversation. The house was so quiet that she could actually hear the voice on the other line. It was Dentry, calling with information.

"We looked everywhere, sir," Dentry said. "The only listing we could find for anyone by the name of Mark Riley was a man that died in 1977. It's a fake name, sir. Probably a fake address, too."

"I wish it was," Rising said. "Thanks."

He ended the call and Mackenzie realized that all eyes were on her now.

She unfolded the paper, expecting a taunting note of some kind.

What she found, though, was somehow worse. It sent a sickening knot of worry dropping through her stomach.

"What is it?" Ellington asked.

She turned and showed it to him. They read it together with Rising peering over her shoulder.

Bellevue Storage. Unit 32.

There was a crude little smiley face underneath the words. The immature hand behind the drawing and the sloppy handwriting made it appear as if the paper had been left behind by a child.

68

"Holy shit," Mackenzie said. She turned to Rising and asked, "How far away is Bellevue?"

"Fifteen minutes from here. Maybe twelve if we haul ass."

That's exactly what they did as they turned back toward the hall and made their way back through the darkened house.

CHAPTER EIGHTEEN

Once the creepiness of the abandoned house and the doll it had been hiding had worn off, both Mackenzie and Ellington were able to properly appreciate the fact that they now seemed to be on to something. Granted, they were only on to something because someone—presumably the killer—had left a hint for them, but it was better than nothing.

"I just don't get it," Ellington said from behind the wheel. They were once again following Rising, this time out to Bellevue. "Let's assume that doll and the paper were left there by the killer. Why in the hell would he want to help us?"

It was the same question that had been eating at Mackenzie. She had a theory that felt right but also a little complicated. "I still think it's all about the tea party theme. He's setting something up. Getting ready for something. Waiting. Apparently, we aren't moving fast enough for him. He's using this to push us along."

"So you think he *wants* to get caught?"

"I don't know. It *feels* like it. But if he wanted to get caught, he would have been leaving little notes like that for us all along."

They both mulled this over in their own way. As Mackenzie sorted through her own thoughts, she felt like she had been running at full speed all day. Had she really been in Oregon that morning? Had she really only been back in Seattle for five hours?

"So my mother called today," Ellington said. "Twice."

"She still in DC waiting on you to get back?"

"No. She went home. Said she didn't really care for the venue we'd chosen after all. She thought it was too generic."

Mackenzie shrugged. "If you don't care what she thinks, then neither will I. I do have to wonder, though…is that a relationship I'm going to have to make myself have?"

"You mean between you and my mother?"

Mackenzie nodded. It felt silly to be talking about such things in the face of what they were currently doing but it did, at least, help to keep her alert. It also kept her from overthinking the facts of the case.

"I don't care. She's beyond help these days. Anyone and everyone pisses her off. If my wife is among those she doesn't like, so be it."

"Has she flat out said she doesn't like me?"

"Not in so many words. But I've told her about your dedication to your work and she thinks work should not be a wife's main priority."

"Did you use the word *dedication*?" she asked.

"No. Actually I used the term *over-committed*. I thought she'd appreciate that."

Mackenzie wasn't quite sure why, but that remark hurt a bit. She frowned and asked: "You think I over-commit?"

"Sometimes. There are days where it seems that work is the only thing on your heart and mind."

"Is that a bad thing?"

"I thought it might be at first. But it's one of the things I like about you. I should say, though, that I've seen you softening. The little looks you gave me back at that house, wanting me to kick the door down. It was nice to see that side of you on the job…even if it *was* a little embarrassing."

"Embarrassing?" She was starting to feel like this was one of those conversations they should have stopped having about thirty seconds ago. She was getting tired, they were both under a lot of stress, and sometimes Ellington didn't know when to stop talking.

"Yeah…right in front of Rising. It didn't seem appropriate to be flirting."

"That wasn't flirting," Mackenzie said.

"Seemed like it. Felt like it. It's just…"

"What?"

He shrugged. "It makes me understand why McGrath was so hesitant to send us out together on this. Maybe we *can't* work together without the feelings getting in the way."

In that moment, Mackenzie felt that he might as well have reached over and slapped her in the face. He hadn't worried about such things when they had only been sleeping together. True, they had both seemed to gradually grow more protective of each other while on the job as their relationship had developed, but she had seen that as a positive aspect of their partnership.

Has he been seeing it as a negative this whole time? she wondered.

"And now I've pissed you off, huh?" he said.

"No comment. Let's just focus on the job. And please don't take that as me being over-committed."

"Ah, Jesus…Mackenzie."

She shook her head curtly. It was another of their little signals to one another—her way of telling him to drop it now before she got *really* angry.

71

Up ahead, Rising was giving his turn signal. Mackenzie waited with anxiousness, suddenly wanting to get out of the car as soon as possible.

***

Mackenzie stepped out of the car without saying a word to Ellington. She watched as Rising approached the front office to Bellevue Storage. It was a small one-room building, protected by an electric key pad.

"The owner was very understanding and cooperative when I called him," Rising said. "Gave me the code to get into his office for the spare key. He was hesitant at first but he'd gotten wind of the murder at Seattle Storage Solutions and seemed to be very concerned. He was so scared about a bad public image, I think he might have given me the deed to the place if I'd asked for it."

Rising tapped in the numbers carefully, clearly respecting the privacy of the owner.

"He staying away from the potential crime scene?" Mackenzie asked.

"No. He's on the way down right now just in case we need anything else."

Mackenzie waited by the door as Rising went inside to retrieve the key to Unit 32. Ellington stepped up beside her but didn't bother trying to say anything. The tension between them was thick, almost like a physical presence between them. Ellington knew her well enough to let the issue set for a while longer, especially now that they were potentially on the brink of making a discovery regarding this case.

Rising came out with the key and the three of them started walking down the paved grounds. It was a nicer outdoor facility, the units well cared for and spaced apart a few feet so that each unit wasn't right on top of its neighboring units. There were two street lamps, one on either side of the lot that contained the units. It did a fair job of lighting the area, but not quite enough to set Mackenzie's mind at ease. She took her Maglite out once again and trailed it along the front sides of the units. When she did, she saw that they were separated almost like houses along a street. Even numbers were on the right, odd on the left.

Unit 32 came into view twenty seconds later. As they passed by Unit 30, Mackenzie stopped. She sniffed the air and started to worry.

"What is it?" Ellington asked.

Rising took another step forward and then he stopped too. "Damn."

Something smelled foul up ahead. Mackenzie tried her best to imagine what it might be other than a dead body but she knew that was exactly what it was. It was similar to the smell that had been reported to Quinn Tuck before he had discovered the body of Claire Locke. Mackenzie had smelled it before as well, a few different times on different cases. It was a smell you never quite forgot.

"Need me to open it?" Mackenzie asked Rising.

The deputy shook his head and stepped forward. He slid the key into the lock and turned it. The *click* of the lock releasing seemed impossibly loud in the silence of the night. Almost instinctually, Mackenzie checked her watch. It had somehow gotten to be 12:16.

Ellington grabbed the little handle at the bottom of the roll-up door and slid it up.

Before it was open even a quarter of the way, the smell came rolling out in waves. Mackenzie cringed and shielded her nose and mouth with the crook of her elbow. Rising wasn't quite as skilled at containing himself. He let out a little moan, turned away from the agents, and puked.

"My God," Ellington said, taking a step back.

He looked to Mackenzie and shot her a glance that seemed to ask: *Are you okay?* The argument they'd had in the car was now on hold.

Mackenzie nodded and aimed her light into the unit.

It was almost entirely empty. There were three plastic bins in the back, along with a cheap-looking safe. Mackenzie spotted a small cup of some kind sitting on the floor in front of the bins but she looked away from it quickly.

The body lying a few feet from the open door was much more deserving of her attention.

It was a woman, clothed in a T-shirt with a band name on it and a pair of jean shorts that rode pretty high. There was dried blood in her short-cropped blonde hair. She was lying on her side, as if to make sure to greet whoever opened her unit door. Because she was looking directly at them, Mackenzie could tell right away that this woman had been here for a very long time.

It was more than the smell, which was still hard to deal with. It was also the look of her skin. It was pale and started to decay. Mackenzie guessed the body had been here for at least a month. Maybe more.

73

A single stab wound had been placed high in her stomach. Her hands were tied behind her back and her ankles had been bound together. A thick belt had been clamped around her mouth, pressing a white cloth down into her mouth.

For the first time in her run as an agent, Mackenzie had to look away. She'd seen dead bodies before—even partially decayed ones—but this was different somehow. This woman was dressed. This woman had been placed here on purpose, left to die and be found like some weird little scavenger hunt.

She'd been used, discarded, and forgotten. Worst of all, the fact that she was apparently not part of the missing persons list they had compiled earlier in the night meant that she had no one in her life who had cared or noticed that she had gone missing. And even if someone *had* noticed, they had not cared enough to check up on her.

"Mac," Ellington said. "Step outside. It's okay."

Not that she needed his approval, but she took his advice. When she stepped outside, Rising looked at her with an embarrassed expression. "Sorry," he said. "It kind of snuck up on me."

Mackenzie only nodded as she collected her breath and her thoughts. Somehow, the night seemed even quieter than it had when they had arrived. And, of course, as she looked up into the cloudy sky, a spitting of rain started to fall.

***

The owner of the complex arrived ten minutes later. By then, Mackenzie had collected herself well enough to head back inside. Rising ran to the main office to meet the owner, just to let him know what was going on—and to suggest that he not come out there with them. Rising had seemed more than happy to be the one to get that particular task.

Mackenzie knew that the body might have many answers to offer but they'd mostly be discovered by the coroner. This was the logic she used to look beyond the rotting body and take a look at what else was in the unit.

She immediately checked out the little cup she thought she'd seen. It was sitting in front of one of the bins. It had cute little flowers painted on it. Written in red letters was the word SUGAR. Like the teapot they had found in Elizabeth Newcomb's unit, it was very small—likely part of a child's tea set.

"You were right," Ellington said. "He's been waiting. Waiting for us to catch up. Jesus…how many more do you think there are?"

She thought about it for a minute, thinking back to something Janell Harper had told them about the mindset of their killer. "I think this might be it," she answered. "Or at least the only one he'd killed before Claire Locke. If there were more and he was indeed getting impatient with us, that slip of paper would have had several other units on it, too."

"Unless it's not just that he's waiting," Ellington said. "Maybe all of it is a game to him. He's showing us a playful side by leaving the fucking tea set everywhere. And the doll. Maybe he's playing some kind of a game with us, too."

Mackenzie didn't think this was the case. There was something desperate about the way he was splitting up the elements of the tea party. It had the feel of a kid who wanted to play, but didn't know how to go about making friends. She kept this to herself for the moment, though; the last thing she wanted was to drive a wedge even farther between them.

They opened up each bin one by one, hoping to find something else. They worked quickly, an unspoken agreement between them to get the hell away from the stench of the body as quickly as possible.

There wasn't much of anything in the bins. One of them did contain a few old fliers and promotional booklets for outlet stores. There were some for Old Navy and a few for Pottery Barn. The name on the address label was Lindsay Nettles. Mackenzie wanted to assume this would be the woman currently lying on the concrete floor, but given the way this case had been going, she just didn't know.

As she looked through the third bin, rummaging past a few paperback books and old CDs, there was a light knock on the side of the unit. She looked up and saw Rising standing there rather timidly.

"Agents, I spoke to the owner just now. He's looking through the paperwork. I think you might want to hear what he's been telling me."

Glad to be done with the unit for now, Mackenzie and Ellington followed Rising back to the little office building. The moist night air smelled like heaven as far as Mackenzie was concerned. It was refreshing, but the scent of the body still clung to the inside of her nostrils.

They entered the office as the owner was digging through a drawer in a small filing cabinet that sat behind the counter. He looked over his shoulder as they entered and gave them a sleepy smile.

"Hey there," he said. "I'm Leroy Johnson. I've been running this place for the last three years and I have *never* seen anything like what Deputy Rising was telling me you found."

"You hadn't smelled anything over the last few days?" Ellington asked.

"I thought I did three days ago," Leroy said. "Just a light whiff, though. But every now and again, someone will hit a skunk out in the road, or even a stupid deer that gets lost and ends up in the middle of the road. It's rare, but it happens. I thought that was all it was. Didn't even think about it again."

"Tell them what you told me," Rising said. "About the man."

Leroy pulled a sheet of paper from the cabinet, shut the drawer, and then gave his full attention to Mackenzie and Ellington.

"The deputy was telling me that you found a woman's body in that unit," Leroy said. "He also told me about the case you're working on, finding women in their storage units. But Unit 32 did not belong to a woman."

"You're sure?" Mackenzie asked.

"Certain of it," he said, handing her the paper he had taken out of the cabinet. "I even remember this guy. Tall drink of water, with dark hair. Had a bandage over his nose, right across the bridge."

Mackenzie looked at the paper. It was an application to rent one of the units. She scanned the paper and came to the name and signature. She furrowed her brow and showed it to Ellington.

"Mark Riley," he read. "But right there…the address on this is different than the one we visited earlier."

Mackenzie had noticed this, too, but wasn't sure it meant anything. Maybe this asshole *was* just toying with them.

"Can you look to see if you have any units rented out to Lindsay Nettles?"

"Sure. One second."

He went back through his filing cabinet, looking for the information. It was one of those times where Mackenzie did *not* see the appeal in doing things the old, simpler way. An Excel spreadsheet on a computer and they'd have the information in one second.

But Leroy only took about twenty seconds. He pulled a file and showed it to them. "Lindsay Nettles. She's been renting a unit for about six months now. Unit number 36."

Mackenzie handed Lindsay's application to Rising. "You know where this address is right off the top of your head?"

"Lovingston," he said. "It's probably about a thirty-minute drive from here...maybe twenty from Seattle. Little no-name town."

"Can you plug this address into your GPS?" she asked. "And then place the call to your department about the body. I need the coroner out here ASAP. I'm going to go get a look at Lindsay Nettles's unit."

Having anticipated this, Leroy had already taken the spare key from his inventory. He tossed the key over the counter to Mackenzie.

"This floors me," Leroy said. "And now that I think of it, there was a man last week that went into his unit. Came in here and said he thought he smelled something kind of foul. But I didn't think anything of it. Didn't even bother going out to look into it."

"Don't start doing that," Mackenzie said. "You can't place any of the blame on yourself. There's no way you could have known."

She took the key and wasted no time heading back outside. As she passed by the unit that had been signed out to Mark Riley, she only glanced into it. The smell was just as bad, even with the door having been open for about ten minutes.

Mackenzie unlocked Unit 36 and drew the door up. She wasn't sure what she was going to find, but she was sure it couldn't be worse than what they had found two units down. When the door was rolled up, an automated light came on overhead. It shone down on the contents of Unit 36 and Mackenzie found herself holding her breath.

At first glance, there was nothing there. A few cardboard boxes, an old writing desk, and a crate of old tools. Nothing out of the ordinary.

So why go through the trouble of moving three of her bins into his unit?

It made no sense...unless it was the killer's way of helping them identify the body and directing them to her unit.

She stepped inside and looked around. As she did, she saw a doll sitting on the floor between a crate and a cardboard box. Unable to help herself, Mackenzie picked it up. It looked eerily similar to the one they had found in the abandoned house. This one had a little tea cup taped to its hand.

Fuming, Mackenzie tossed the doll to the ground. She kicked it, feeling juvenile when she realized it felt incredibly good. Still, as she stormed back out of the unit, she could not shake the feeling that the damned doll was watching her leave.

Smiling at her, even...like it knew a secret.

CHAPTER NINETEEN

Mackenzie was starting to feel as if they were being toyed with. It was bad enough that despite the number of scenes the killer had visited, they still had no real leads. But now that it seemed that he had them on some strange cat-and-mouse chase that he was very much in charge of, Mackenzie was starting to get pissed off.

It was 1:34 in the morning as she and Ellington turned off of the main highway, onto the secondary feeder road. The address they had taken from Leroy's application had pointed them here. Deputy Rising had confirmed that there were indeed several houses back in a small thicket of woods down this road. He had then called a few officers to join him at Bellevue Storage to go over the two units in question.

As Ellington drove them further down the road, Mackenzie became more and more certain that they'd find a house just as abandoned as the first one. The question was whether or not the killer had elected to leave them any eerie clues at this location.

"Forgive me for saying so," Ellington said, "but it looks like something's eating at you. I truly apologize if the whole discussion with my mother pissed you off."

"It wasn't the part about your mother," she said. "It was how you described me. But—and don't take this the wrong way—I couldn't care less about what you think of me right now. I'd much rather just try to close this fucking case."

The car went quiet. It was rare that Mackenzie used such an expletive and whenever she did, it seemed to rattle Ellington. Apparently, he decided that it would be best to simply let her stew in it for a while longer because he did not try to break through to her again.

The address came up on their right in the form of a long driveway that appeared to be a gravel road. In the approaching glow of headlights, it looked like an expanse that simply opened up into the forest and then swallowed the road entirely.

The driveway went down a small hill and then came to a stop at an aluminum carport. An old Civic sat beneath it. To the left of the carport stood a simple one-story house, the kind that reminded of Mackenzie of the shack-like structures in larger cities that were the types of places people on government housing assistance lived.

There were no lights on inside the house. As they stepped out of the car, everything around them was quiet and still.

They shared an uneasy look over the hood of the car. Both of them unholstered their sidearms as they started toward the house. Mackenzie waited until they reached the porch to switch on her Maglite, not wanting to take the chance of alerting anyone who might be inside.

On the porch, she tried the front doorknob just for the hell of it. When it turned easily in her hand and the door swung open, she expected the worst: a man waiting with a gun, pointing directly at them; a dead body on the floor; a trap. But there was nothing of the sort. There was only the interior of a house.

But unlike the previously deserted one, this one had been lived in. For all she knew, someone was asleep in a bedroom down the hall to her right even as they entered. But as Mackenzie slowly moved through the living room, she could sense that they were alone. It was another of those innate talents that had come over the past two years working as an agent. Yes, this house had been lived in, but no one had been here for quite some time.

The living room was small, containing a small couch, a TV stand holding an older model television, and a coffee table littered with empty soda cans, used napkins, and…

"Shit," Ellington breathed.

He had spotted the other items on the coffee table as well.

Three tea cups, all sitting in a triangular shape.

Mackenzie put a finger to her mouth, the universal *hush* gesture. She then pointed to the hallway, assuming there was a bedroom there. Yes, her hunch told her that they were alone but her hunches had been wrong in the past.

They walked quietly down the hallway. The place was empty. No pictures on the walls, no decorations of any kind in the hallway. There was a bathroom on the left, and a linen closet beside that. There were two bedrooms side by side on the right side of the hallway. The doors to both were open. The first held a bed, a bedside table, and a clock. The closet was open, revealing just a few crumpled T-shirts and a pair of pants.

Might be able to get some prints or something off of those, Mackenzie thought.

They ventured into the other bedroom and when they turned on the light, Mackenzie's heart skipped a beat.

There were several boxes and bins pushed against the far wall. In front of each one was a doll or some sort of tea party paraphernalia.

Mackenzie walked over to the boxes and plucked the top of the first one open. She peered inside and all saw all manner of dolls. They were dirty and scarred, their hair matted. Some of them were missing eyes or appendages.

"This has officially gotten creepy," she said.

Ellington popped open the next box and peered inside, Mackenzie looked over his shoulder and saw a collection of teapots, tea kettles, tea cups, and little ornate play snacks—crackers, little cakes, fruit, and pastries. Most of the pots, cups, and kettles were wrapped in bubble wrap or plastic sheeting. Still, there were fragments of a few that had broken and shattered.

"How's he living here under a fake name?" Mackenzie wondered out loud.

"Ten bucks says he rents it," Ellington replied. "It would be much easier to use a fake name that way. Still, I'd like to talk to the person that owns this property."

"We should get Rising to look into that."

They checked the other boxes and bins—two more boxes and three bins—and found more of the same. Tucked inside one of the bins was a decorative tablecloth and picnic blanket.

With the contents of each package checked, they headed back throughout the house. Ellington checked the bathroom and kitchen while Mackenzie looked over the bedroom. The bed was unmade and she knew there would be stray hairs in it. But without anything to compare them to—say, from one of the crime scenes, it would ultimately do no good. Still, she made a mental note to come back in with an evidence kit to collect any loose hairs or other detritus such as dead skin or even bodily fluids.

She met Ellington as he was coming out of the kitchen. "Anything?" she asked.

"Nothing. The medicine cabinet is empty, with the exception of a bottle of Motrin. No prescriptions with a name. No mail anywhere that I can see, either. It makes me think he doesn't *live* here."

"Maybe he brings the victims here at some point."

"Why would he do that?" Ellington asked.

She thought of the boxes of dolls and tea party staples in the back bedroom. "To play," she said.

They exited the house quickly. The hour was getting very late and they had been yanked around enough. Mackenzie popped the trunk to the car to retrieve the evidence kit while Ellington pulled out his phone to dial up Rising for an information request on who the house belonged to.

As Mackenzie leaned into the trunk, something to the left caught her eye. For a moment, her hand went back to her Glock before she realized that it was not a person, but a structure. It was out there, at the edge of the woods, fairly small. She took her flashlight back out and pointed the beam in that direction.

"Got something?" Ellington said, his fingers paused in pulling up Rising's number.

"Just a doghouse," she said.

But that wasn't quite right. It wasn't *just* a doghouse.

She walked slowly toward it, feeling certain there was no danger there but hesitant all the same. When she was standing directly in front of it, she knelt down and shined her light inside.

A length of old chain, maybe once belonging to an actual dog, was coiled in a perfect circle in the center. A single ceramic teapot sat in the middle. Positioned around the circle of chain sat three dolls. One stared directly out of the doghouse, its dead black eyes glaring right at Mackenzie.

Ellington stepped up behind her and hunched down as well. "Jesus," he said. "Do you think based on what we're seeing here we can start to assume the killer is at least a little crazy?"

It was a tempting thought to consider, but there had to be a lot of planning and meticulous detail involved to get them to go along on this little chase. If he *was* mentally unstable, he also had a vast set of strengths to compensate.

"Let's get out of here," Mackenzie said.

She got to her feet and turned back for the car without waiting to see if Ellington was following. Yet when she was back in the car and Ellington was pulling out several seconds later, she could not help but look back out to that doghouse. She could not see the dolls any longer, but God help her, she felt like she could sense their lifeless eyes on her all the same.

CHAPTER TWENTY

Mackenzie fell into bed at 2:35 with no clear idea of how tomorrow would go. Rising assured them that they'd know who owned the property with the creepy doghouse and possibly even have spoken with him by the time they woke up the following morning.

After what she had witnessed and experienced the night before, Mackenzie desperately wanted a shower. But a mix of a long day and several surges of fear-induced adrenaline had wiped her out. She barely managed to strip out of her clothes before slipping under the covers.

Ellington moved a bit slower as he readied himself for bed. He seemed lost in thought, a pensive look in his eyes as he brushed his teeth. Mackenzie considered asking him what was bothering him aside from their argument but decided against it. She was just too damned tired.

She had just drifted off to sleep when Ellington slid into bed. She could tell that he was intentionally trying to keep his distance. She respected his decision and was glad that he was able to read her so well but at the same time, she badly wanted to be held. Something about this case was stirring something quite deep inside of her. And although it would take a bit of prodding and discussion for Ellington to draw it out of her, she knew that he could tell.

She nearly rolled over to him and took him in her arms. In light of all of the death they were dealing with as of late, some stupid argument about the way he'd described her to his mother seemed utterly foolish.

But the day had taken its toll on her and she was drifting off to sleep before she could so much as roll over onto her side.

***

She stirred awake at the sound of the door opening. She tensed up and nearly sprang out of bed before hearing Ellington's voice.

"It's just me," he said. "Sorry I woke you. I went out and grabbed breakfast."

She glanced to the clock and saw that it was 7:37. In her own personal view, this was far too late to sleep—particularly when they were in the middle of a case. But after how yesterday went down, she felt she deserved it.

She rolled out of bed and joined Ellington at the small table by the window. He had grabbed a few sausage biscuits and a parfait from McDonald's, as well as two coffees. As she took one of the biscuits, she checked her phone.

"Nothing from Rising on the owner of the house?" she asked.

"Not yet."

She sipped from the coffee, smiling at the fact that Ellington knew her so well. A splash of cream and a ton of sugar. Just how she liked it.

"I've been thinking," Ellington said. "The dolls and the tea party stuff...could the killer be placing them in the units just to throw us off? Maybe to just add another layer to what might be an otherwise simple case?"

"He could be. But then that rules out your comment last night of him being potentially crazy."

"If you think about it, the dolls are almost generic. Creepy dolls are a pretty common trope of horror these days. He may as well just carve some pumpkins and paint BOO on the inside of the units."

"That's exactly why I *don't* think they're there just to throw us off," Mackenzie said. "Why go through the trouble of using something so cliché and generic?"

"You know," he said, "I was thinking about something else, too. Our argument yesterday. I really don't know why you—"

The ringing of her phone interrupted him. She thought it might be a good thing, too. The tone in his voice and the way the sentence had started made her feel like he was going to be defensive and try to blame her.

Pushing these feelings to the side, she answered her phone. "This is Agent White."

"Agent White, it's Deputy Rising. I think you might want to come out to Osborne Storage," he said. "A smaller little business just outside of the city."

"You find something?"

"Yeah," Rising said, his voice low. "Another body."

CHAPTER TWENTY ONE

When they arrived at Osborne Storage, the sun was peeking through the clouds. Mackenzie was pretty sure it was the first time she'd seen genuine sunlight since they'd arrived in Seattle. She'd managed to grab a quick shower before leaving the motel; that, combined with the sunshine, had her feeling uplifted and positive.

It was a fleeting feeling, though. Rising met them at the entrance to the front gate of Osborne Storage. He had not been exaggerating when he'd said the place was tiny. It had only a dozen units and while they looked relatively new, the grounds they were located on were in need of some maintenance. The units sat in the center of a gravel lot that was bordered on all sides by undeveloped fields.

There was a man standing with Rising, a tall older gentleman who looked like he might jump right out of his skin at any moment. He looked very uncomfortable as Mackenzie and Ellington approached.

"Agents, this is Barry Osborne, the owner of Osborne Storage," Rising said. "He came out this morning to open up and do some maintenance. Mr. Osborne, do you want to tell them the rest?"

Osborne nodded, anxious to get his story out. "Like he said, I came out early because I try to make the place look presentable at least once a week. I was going to do some weed eating around the edges and sweep up at the unit entrances. I was sweeping up when I came to Unit Five. I saw something sort of seeping out from under the door. I knew what it was but just didn't want to believe it, you know?"

"What was it?" Mackenzie asked, already knowing the answer.

"Blood."

"Thanks, Mr. Osborne," Rising said. "You mind if me and the agents take it from here?"

"Please do," Osborne said. "If you need me, I'll be in the office."

Osborne took his leave, looking quite happy to do so. Rising then led Mackenzie and Ellington across the gravel lot. Each unit had a small concrete loading area, ramped at an angle to make moving heavy things in on dollies and carts much easier. She could see where Osborne had swept up around the first four ramps. And

84

then, just as he had said, there was something dark and sticky coming out from beneath the door of Unit 5.

It was unmistakably blood.

"You haven't opened it yet?" Ellington asked.

"Oh no. I wanted you two here first. Mr. Osborne has already unlocked it for us, though." He reached down and grabbed the handle. "Ready?"

Mackenzie and Ellington nodded in unison.

Rising lifted the door and revealed the inside of the unit. It was easily the most cluttered one they had seen, though it was still stacked and organized in a fairly consistent manner. There was about seven feet of space between the entrance and where the boxes began. Lying on the floor of that space was a blonde female, her face turned toward them.

"The blood is fresh," Ellington said.

Mackenzie nodded and, feeling the slightest glimmer of hope, she knelt by the body and felt for a pulse along the neck. There was no pulse but she found the flesh almost warm.

"She hasn't been dead for long," she said.

She looked to the blood on the floor, trying to figure out how it had ended up seeping out from under the door. It looked as if the floor wasn't perfectly level. It wasn't too hard to accept, given that the state of the entire place was a little shoddy. Mackenzie assumed the units here were much less pricey than ones at a place like Bellevue Storage or U-Store-It. And you apparently got what you paid for.

"This might be our killer's first oversight," Mackenzie said.

"What's that?" Ellington asked.

"The floor here isn't level. The blood flows down a very gradual slope towards the door. If the floor were level here, there's no telling how much time might have passed before someone discovered her body."

Ellington got down on his haunches and cocked his head, looking at the floor. "Yeah, I see it. Shit…it's so fresh it's still pooling out. If Osborne had gotten here an hour earlier…maybe…"

"I don't know," Mackenzie said. "This is a lot of blood. It makes me wonder if the killer is in a hurry now. He's allowed the others at least a little bit of time to suffer…to maybe even starve to death. So why not this one?"

She didn't expect an answer, nor did she get one. As they both looked to the lightly downward angle of the blood flow, Rising stepped into the unit. "Agents," he said, nodding toward the back of the unit.

Mackenzie followed the direction of his nod and saw two little dolls sitting together on top of one of the boxes. One looked rather new while the other had clearly seen some rough times.

"Any cameras in this place?" Ellington asked.

"None," Rising said. "As you can probably guess from the state of the place, Mr. Osborne is clearly not sinking much money into the care or maintenance of the place."

"We need to get an ID on the body," Mackenzie said. "And then an address. My guess is that she hasn't been dead for more than three or four hours. That means she was dumped here less than a day or so ago. This might be the first time we'll be able to trace any sort of path the killer might have made."

"Well," Rising said, "we can't use any bank transactions to find out an ID. Osborne accepts cash only."

"Damn," Ellington said. "Can we just catch one single break?"

"What's the name on the application for the unit?" Mackenzie asked.

"I didn't ask," Rising said.

A voice spoke up from outside of the unit. "The application is under the name Mark Riley."

The voice was Osborne's. He'd apparently elected to stay behind and watch from a distance rather than return to the office as he had originally said.

Mackenzie looked at Ellington and saw that he was getting frustrated. She was, too. In fact, she was quickly growing livid. With units paid for in cash and a fake name at each one, there was no telling how long this guy would remain free.

"You ever meet this Mark Riley guy?" Mackenzie asked Osborne.

"Once, about a year or so ago. When he filled out the application. He pays regularly, but it's always with cash, in an envelope that comes through the mail. I thought it was weird, so I checked the return address one time and it's just the central Seattle post office."

"Crazy or not," Ellington said, "this fucker is smart."

She hated to admit such a thing, but Ellington was right: their killer was very smart. No witnesses. No footage, with the exception of the cars coming in and out at the first crime scene—a lead that would take weeks to land a suspect.

"Do you recall what he looked like?" Mackenzie asked.

"I don't, I'm sorry."

Mackenzie stepped out of the unit and then looked back inside, trying to see it in the same way the killer might see it. What was the appeal? Why was he using these units?

"Mr. Rising, can you get some officers to go through these boxes?"

"Sure," Rising said.

Ellington, as if curious to get started, opened the lid of the one closest to him. He peered inside and shrugged. "Shredded paper. It's like the boxes are just stage dressing or something." He went to the next one, opened it, and chuckled. "Unopened rolls of toilet paper," he said. He gave the box a weak little punch in frustration.

"In the meantime," she said, "we also need to get a list of all storage complexes in Seattle and the surrounding areas. We need to let them all know what's going on. If we don't have a lead in another day or so, we may need to get them all to shut their businesses for a day or so."

"Or we could position an undercover cop at each location," Rising said.

"That's up to the local PD," Mackenzie said. "But even if there's only thirty or so locations, that's using up a lot of resources."

"Well, we have to start somewhere," Ellington said. "This is starting to get out of hand."

"Starting?" Rising asked, defeated.

"I've got two friends that own storage places," Osborne said. He was still keeping a respectable distance from the unit. "I can call them and let them know. Maybe see if they've seen anything alarming as of late."

"Thanks," Mackenzie said.

She looked at the woman's blood on the floor and then at the dolls. Like the ones in the doghouse from last night, these seemed to be staring at her—almost taunting her.

"You okay?" Ellington asked, coming in close to her.

"No."

And with that simple answer, she left the unit. She felt her emotions welling up inside of her—something that never happened to her on the job.

This one is getting under my skin, Mackenzie thought. *If we don't wrap this one up soon, I feel like I'm going to break…*

She wondered if it was the stress of the upcoming wedding or maybe even some resentment that she had buried toward McGrath, making sure she and Ellington knew that this would be their last time working together. She honestly didn't know what it was…why this case was getting to her so badly.

But she felt that if she didn't wrap it up soon, it could very well be the first blemish on what had so far been a remarkable career.

CHAPTER TWENTY TWO

The morning stretched on like she was stuck in some wretched sort of purgatory. The only real information they were able to get came an hour later when the victim was identified as twenty-four-year-old Kelly Higdon of Seattle. Her only local relative was her grandfather, who was currently residing in a retirement home with a severe case of Alzheimer's disease. Seattle PD ran Higdon's record and found it clean.

Because of Higdon's clean record, Mackenzie was not expecting much when they searched her apartment later that morning. She and Ellington entered the place only because it was the single lead they had. Granted, part of Mackenzie almost expected to find some sort of doll or tea party set up in the apartment. But there was nothing.

Ellington surfed through the web browser history of Higdon's laptop while Mackenzie looked the bedroom over. After half an hour of searching, neither of them found anything that was remotely linked to her murder or the storage unit. Just like the storage unit, Higdon's apartment turned up nothing.

Frustrated and more defeated than she had felt on a case in a very long time, Mackenzie knew that the only thing they could do for the remainder of the day was to hole up at the police station and dig into the files. As calls were made to all of the other storage complexes in the city, her hope was that some little detail might come from one of the owners, just the tiniest little nugget that might lead them *somewhere.*

They found themselves back at the station, in the conference room by themselves, trying to talk the case out. It was usually these environments that Mackenzie and Ellington really started firing on all cylinders—in a room together, firing ideas back and forth until something clicked and just made sense. It had happened several times before but within five minutes, they knew that it was not going to be the case this time around. Something just felt off...not only with the case, but between them as well.

"Let's start with the most obvious fact," Mackenzie said, sitting across from Ellington and finding it hard to truly focus on him. "He's renting these units in advance. So I think it's safe to assume he *knew* why he'd be renting them."

"Makes sense, but that could get pretty expensive. We also need to consider, though, that not all of the victims have been found in units under his name. In Claire Locke's case, for example, the unit belonged to her, the victim."

"I'm getting hung up on that, too," Mackenzie said. "But I wonder if maybe that one was just a matter of convenience. It would also indicate that even though he does rent these units, he doesn't feel the need to use them all of the time. There's apparently nothing special about them. He saw an opportunity to easily dispose of a body in a unit that was *right there* and he took it."

"Another thing that's not sitting well with me is the fact that some of the units are basically empty, while others seemed to be almost staged."

"Did Rising ever get back to us about what the police found in the boxes in this latest unit?"

Ellington pulled up a text from Rising on his phone and read it. "It's still in progress, but so far it looks like all filler stuff. Toilet paper, jugs of distilled water, old magazines. Nothing that someone would actually need a storage unit for. No personal belongings, no clutter, nothing like that."

"I agree then," Mackenzie said. "I think the boxes in this last one was like stage dressing. Not quite as symbolic as whatever he's doing with the dolls and teacups, but decoration all the same."

"Yeah, but why?"

"I have no idea," Mackenzie answered. "And that's what's driving me crazy."

Ellington let out a sigh and then got up from his chair. "I'm going to point something out and it's probably going to piss you off."

"Maybe don't point it out then."

Ignoring her, he awkwardly walked around the table toward her. "You took something I said very personally last night. And maybe I'm stupid for not quite realizing why it upset you so much. But whatever it is, it's clearly bothering you. I've never seen you so flustered over a case before. So if the argument we had is to blame for that, I think we need to get to the bottom of it right now."

"I'm about to marry a man who feels that I put way too much attention and focus on my job," she said. "Maybe you meant what you said as a compliment…but to me, a woman who is quite frankly terrified of getting married, it was very off-putting. And if you can't see that about me at this stage, I think I might have been a little too generous in the way I thought you knew me."

"You're *terrified* of marrying me? You've used the word *nervous* before. *Jittery,* too. But this is a new word. And I think it's a pretty strong one."

"Well, it's true."

"When were you going to tell me?"

"I don't know. It came out of nowhere. I think it had something to do with meeting your mother—as briefly as that might have been. It was the first time it actually seemed real."

"Is that a bad thing?"

"No. But it was an *abrupt* thing. It hit me out of nowhere."

Ellington seemed to sit on this for a moment, going through every possible response in his head before responding. "I love you very much, Mackenzie. But if you're getting cold feet, I think that's something we need to address."

"Agreed," she said, angry at herself for being so passive right away. "But first, let's see if we can't wrap this case. Sorry…but it takes priority as far as I'm concerned."

Ellington folded his arms and nodded. "I'm going to get some coffee," he said with a grunt of frustration.

He left the room, closing the door behind him. When it was closed, Mackenzie had to fight the urge to slam her fist down on the table. Why the hell was she being so angry and stubborn to Ellington? She knew very well that he had not meant anything ill by what he had said. And yes, she *was* a little freaked out about the wedding, but she figured that was normal. Wasn't it an almost expected thing for at least one member of the couple to get cold feet as the wedding date approached?

She did her best to wipe all of that out of her mind for the moment. She refused to get distracted when she was working a case that already seemed to be getting the best of her.

She repositioned her focus on the case. There was nothing to really cling to yet, so she tried to imagine why the killer might rent the units so far in advance. How long had he been planning this? And, worse than that, how many units had he rented?

Bingo, she thought.

She reached for her phone, intending to call Rising. If they could get in touch with every local storage complex like they had planned and have them check their records for any units belonging to Mark Riley, they could cut him off before he struck again.

Or could they? There was no guarantee that he was killing his victims *in* the units.

Before she had time to call Rising, Ellington came back into the room. He looked hurried and a bit excited.

91

"We got a hit," he said. "An officer spoke to a storage center five minutes ago...and the owner said there are scratching and moaning noises coming from inside a unit."

Mackenzie instantly got to her feet. "Did they instruct him not to open it?"

"That's been the instruction from the start," Ellington said. "Don't open the unit in case the killer is inside. It wastes some time for us but keeps the owners safe."

"How far away is this center?"

"Fifteen minutes."

They both broke into a run down the hall. And just for that small moment, everything felt exactly right between them again.

CHAPTER TWENTY THREE

The storage facility in question was a generic run-of-the-mill complex. Fifty individual storage sheds with garage-style doors, about twenty by twenty in diameter, sat on a crammed lot. When Mackenzie and Ellington arrived, the gates had been closed and locked, as the police had been calling around and instructing the owners to do. A man—presumably the owner—stood behind them pacing while speaking to someone on his phone. When he saw Mackenzie and Ellington pull up and park, he ended the call and unlocked the gates.

"Is there still movement in the unit?" Mackenzie asked as they got out. She didn't even bother with introductions or formalities. They were on a clock, potentially rushing toward a unit to save a life. She had gone so far to as to call for an ambulance as she and Ellington had raced over.

"Yeah," the owner said. "I heard it no more than two minutes ago."

"Which one?" Ellington asked.

"Unit Seven, down on the right. I already went ahead and unlocked it for you."

They ran at a full sprint down the concrete passage between the two rows of units. As they drew close to Unit 7, Mackenzie drew her Glock. Maybe…just maybe, they had caught the killer in the act.

But her instincts started to sense that this wasn't the case. After all, the gates had been locked for a while now and there appeared to be no cars other than the owner's on the property. Still, potentially saving a life was more than enough. Feeling a little silly, she holstered her sidearm as they came to the door of Unit 7.

Even as Ellington reached down for the door's handle, Mackenzie could hear the sound of movement inside. A series of little thuds and long scratching noises. The scratching sounds were almost paralyzing—the equivalent of nails down a chalkboard.

"If you can hear me," Ellington said, "I need you to step away from the door. This is the FBI and we're coming in!"

The noises stopped, causing Mackenzie and Ellington to share a hopeful glance. With a heave upward, Ellington rolled the door up. Mackenzie eyes went to the floor right away, expecting another crimson pool of blood, another woman needlessly maimed.

But there was nothing.

"What the hell?" Ellington asked.

But even as the question came out of his mouth, they both saw the movement to the left. Mackenzie wheeled in that direction, again going for her sidearm. As her hand fell on the butt of the Glock, embarrassment slammed into her like a rock.

"Are you fucking kidding me?" she asked.

A raccoon went scampering out through the opened doorway. Ellington had apparently been caught unawares well because he took a surprised step backward, also reaching for his sidearm.

Mackenzie watched as the creature went running elsewhere along the property. She wished she could chuckle about it, that it was a story she might pull out later in her career for a good laugh. But as she stood there in the doorway of the storage unit, she felt an anger that was unlike any other she had ever felt.

Two memories flashed through her mind. She thought of the Scarecrow Killer, the very first case that had truly gotten under her skin back before she'd been with the bureau—when she'd still been a detective out in Kansas. And then she thought of meeting with her mother in the employee break room of a motel, moments before finally closing the case on who had killed her father.

She'd felt rage in those moments, of course. But what she felt as she caught the last glimpse of that raccoon scurrying out into the road—where she hoped it would get obliterated by a tractor trailer—dwarfed those emotions.

Mackenzie felt herself clenching her fists as she walked back up the concrete walkway toward the gates. The owner was still there, his gaze now following after the raccoon that had made its escape.

"Oh my God," he said as Mackenzie came by. "I had no idea. I'm sorry. Damned thing was even making some kind of a mewling sound, too. Sounded just like a woman, but quiet."

Mackenzie heard his words but ignored them. She went directly for the car and waited for Ellington. She watched him as he neared the car. The look on his face made it clear that he had been just as embarrassed as she had. But she was taking it personally, and she didn't know why.

As if to put an exclamation point on the day's events as well as her mood, a faint drizzle of rain started to pelt the windshield.

Mackenzie closed her eyes and tried to concentrate on her breathing.

Why is this case bothering me so much? Why am I devouring Ellington with my anger every time we have a conversation?

Suddenly, in the further recesses of her mind, a thought occurred to her. She opened her eyes again, pulling that thought to the surface.

She thought she might know why she was taking the case so hard and why she was simply not letting Ellington off so easily.

It was just a hunch, but it was something.

And facing that would be worse than the continuous rain, worse than any argument she or Ellington might ever have.

She closed her eyes again as a knot of worry started to form in her stomach.

CHAPTER TWENTY FOUR

He knew everything had been far too easy up to this point. He would have been naïve to think it could have kept continuing at this pace. At some point, he was going to hit a snag. And as he watched the people get out of the car from the grimy window of his shed, he saw that snag.

How had he not prepared for this? Of course a woman wasn't going to come to this part of town without some sort of protection. And in this case, that protection was a man. The man, honestly, wasn't much to fear, though. He was fairly short and a little overweight. As he and the woman neared the shed, the man looked around suspiciously. He said something and they both laughed nervously.

Before they could figure out that something might be up, he opened up the shed door—not the roll-up door, but the plain old wooden door that led in and out. He greeted them with a smile and a wave. He knew he had an innocent sort of look, a look that would not raise any alarm in most people. The fact that this woman had contacted him about possibly buying some antique dolls from an ad on Craigslist probably upped the harmless factor.

"Thanks for coming out all this way," he said as they neared the shed. "I have a truck and would have been happy to bring them to you, but the engine started acting up last week and I haven't been able to afford to fix it."

"Not a problem," the girl said.

The man—a boyfriend, he assumed—stepped between them and offered his hand. "I'm Brian," the boyfriend said.

He gave Brian his name and shook his hand. He then led the couple inside the shed. He'd had the place for three years now, purchased at an auction when some failed real state jerk-off had died. He'd used it for several things over time—practicing with his now-defunct band, sleeping out of when he had been homeless for few months last year, and, most recently, to store some of his dolls and teapots and accessories.

"Forgive me for asking…" the woman said. Her name was Daisy Walker and he didn't think much of her. Honestly…who shopped around on Craigslist anymore?

"Ask away," he said.

"How'd you end up with so many old dolls?"

"My aunt," he lied. "She held on to all of her old dolls, hoping she'd pass them down to a daughter. But she never had a daughter. When my aunt passed away, she passed them down to me in her will. No idea why. It was like some cruel joke."

He led them to the back of the shed where the plastic bins were stacked in rows of four, two bins high. He selected the one he needed and pulled it down. He removed the lid and allowed her to look inside.

"What do you need them for, if you don't mind me asking?"

"We're going to go all out for Halloween this year," she said.

"So you want the grungier ones, I guess?"

"Probably," she said.

"Well, take your pick. I just want to get rid of them, so I can cut you a great deal."

She seemed pleased with this, as she started looking into the bins right away. Her boyfriend didn't seem to be very involved but watched as she sifted through the dolls.

He watched them both from the corner of his eye as he pretended to be busy with something at the makeshift workbench on the other side of the shed. He moved quietly, humming to himself, trying to be a non-factor to them. When he was certain that both of their backs were turned to him, he slipped the flat-headed screw driver into the pouch of the hooded sweatshirt he was wearing.

"Hey, how much would you sell a whole bin for?" Daisy called out.

"I don't know," he said, walking slowly over to them. "Ten bucks? Does that sound fair?"

"Yeah, that sounds great," Daisy said. She then looked to her boyfriend and gave him a dainty smile. "Pay the man, please."

The boyfriend frowned and reached for his wallet. As his head tilted down the slightest bit, that's when the screwdriver came out of the pouch pocket.

He drove the flat-headed end of it into the base of the boyfriend's neck. He drove it in with harsh force, creating a popping noise as it tore through the flesh.

The jettison of blood was immediate. It gushed out, as the screwdriver had torn through the carotid artery. The boyfriend staggered back, colliding with Daisy.

He released the screwdriver, knowing full well that even if the boyfriend managed to free the screwdriver and live, he'd only last a minute or so—and he'd certainly not be in any shape to put up much of a fight.

Daisy caught herself on the edge of the bin but as she tried to support herself, the bin went spilling over. This sent her to the floor. She fell with her boyfriend collapsing beside her. His blood was still gushing out, splashing on her bare arms and the floor of the shed. This was unfortunate but nothing to be too concerned about. He'd make sure to clean it as best as he could later.

For now, there was Daisy to worry about.

He removed his hooded sweatshirt and fell down on top of her. He covered her face with the sweatshirt, pressing hard enough to where he could feel the resistance of the concrete floor against her head. Beside them, the boyfriend made a few retching noises, gasping for breath that was blocked by the screwdriver.

He tied the sleeves of the hoodie tight around the back of Daisy's head. He then kicked her hard in the ribs to take the fight out of her.

He stepped back and examined the scene. The entire ordeal had taken less than ten seconds. The boyfriend was nearly motionless and his eyes were going glassy. Daisy, meanwhile, was trying to scream through the sweatshirt.

He thought about taking her back to his house. But that was risky. The feds had already been there. He had led them there, in fact. Soon, he supposed they'd catch on. And they'd be in on his fun.

He smiled as he kicked Daisy again, this time in the stomach. She gasped under the sweatshirt, a sound that made him wonder if she would pass out.

He then went to the farthest bin to the right and opened it up. He reached inside and took out the gags and bailing wire. He looked back at the shape of Daisy's head beneath his sweatshirt.

And then he reached into another bin, pulling out three dolls. He set them up against the bins, facing Daisy.

This was the fun part. He always liked to let his children watch. It motivated him and they seemed to enjoy it.

He spoke to them as he removed the sweatshirt and tightened the ball gag around Daisy's head. He told them all about his plans for Daisy, of how he knew just where he would put the body. And if they were good, he'd let a few of them stay with her to watch her die.

CHAPTER TWENTY FIVE

Mackenzie had never had a panic attack, but she thought this might be what it felt like. Once she and Ellington had returned to the police department, she had made a direct line toward the restroom. She'd heard Ellington calling out for her as they entered the building, but she ignored him. In the restroom, she locked herself in a stall and took a series of long, shaky breaths.

She tried to center her thoughts, to keep herself from slipping into despair.

It's just a hunch, she told herself. *You don't know for sure.*

That was true. But she needed to find out before she pushed too hard against Ellington. In the meantime, maybe she even needed to apologize to him.

Once she felt that she had properly collected herself, she checked herself in the mirror. She looked worn out and defeated; it was the type of paleness that makeup just wasn't going to be able to fix. She turned away from her reflection and headed back out into the department hallway. She made it no more than five steps before Rising caught up with her.

"Just a quick update for you," he said. "Of the fifty-two storage complexes within the city and a grid of twenty-five miles surrounding the city limits, thirty of them have been contacted. Most of them were more than happy to close their gates. There were a few that gave some pushback, though. They refused to close but those that have security cameras agreed to allow us access if needed."

"Can we get a list of the ones that aren't willing to close?" Mackenzie asked.

"Yeah, we're keeping tabs. So far it's only six, though."

"A pretty good percentage. Has anyone bothered to start looking into any recent missing persons cases? Particularly for young women between the ages of eighteen and forty?"

"Yes. We've been keeping tabs on that ever since the second body was discovered."

"Great. Thanks again for the help, Deputy."

"If you don't mind my asking, Agent White…are you okay? You look ill."

"No, I'm good. This case is just getting to me. Have you heard about what we found in that last unit this morning?"

"Raccoon," Rising said. "Yeah. Sorry."

He seemed to take that as his cue to leave her alone. He gave her a little nod of appreciation and broke away from her. Mackenzie, meanwhile, continued down to the conference room. Ellington and three officers were working on the list of storage units, listing them on the whiteboard and then marking them off.

As Mackenzie sat down, she looked at the list and wondered if there was any relevance to the units the killer was using. Was he placing the women in the particular units for a specific reason or was it all random? It might be something worth looking into.

Ellington looked at her and tapped at the board. "The police have already spoken to over half of the local storage complex owners."

"Rising filled me in on my way in," she said. "They're making remarkable progress."

"I'm thinking we need to get at least one police unit over to each of the locations that are refusing to close up shop. It's worth mentioning, though, that out of the locations that are refusing to close, only one of them has a client by the name of Mark Riley. There are already two officers on their way to personally speak with the owner and to canvass the location."

"We're also working on collecting the names of each location that has that name in their files," one of the officers said. "Even if they've agreed to close up until this case is closed."

Mackenzie nodded, though she felt that this was starting to get out of hand. There were lots of moving pieces now. And while that was a good thing, it was also a lot to keep up with—more cracks for things to fall through.

Mackenzie thought about the boxes of dolls at the house they'd searched through. She thought of those dead glassy eyes staring at her from the doghouse. She seriously thought about going back to that house and digging through those boxes. If the killer seemed to find some sort of importance or relevance to the dolls, maybe *that* was where they needed to look. Maybe there was something staring at them—no pun intended—right in the face.

Before she could get a good hold on that thought, the conference room door opened. A very excited-looking Deputy Rising came rushing in.

"A call came in two minutes ago. A concerned mother placed a missing persons report out on her daughter. Twenty-two-year-old Daisy Walker."

Mackenzie was already on her feet when she asked: "Missing since when?"

"At least one o'clock yesterday afternoon."

Mackenzie and Ellington locked eyes across the room. He tossed the dry-erase marker he had been holding to the nearest officer and joined Mackenzie as she headed for the door.

Blood leaking out of a unit and now a fairly warm missing persons case, Mackenzie thought. *If this missing person is related to the killer, he's messing up. He's getting lazy. Or cocky.*

The mere idea of this did nothing more than anger Mackenzie even further. She welcomed it now, using it to fuel her and push her on as she and Ellington headed outside in pursuit of what would hopefully turn out to be a promising lead.

***

When they arrived at the address of Daisy Walker's parents, Mackenzie and Ellington found the mother, Shelby, sitting on the front porch. She was smoking a cigarette with the posture and expression of someone who didn't do it often. Shelby Walker eyed them skeptically as they walked up her sidewalk to the front porch.

"You the police?" she asked.

"FBI," Mackenzie said, showing her ID. "I'm Agent White and this is Agent Ellington."

"Why is the FBI here?" Shelby asked, suddenly more nervous than she had originally appeared. "Is my baby in some sort of trouble?"

"We certainly hope not," Mackenzie said. "If you could answer some questions for us, we can hopefully find out sooner rather than later. We're in town looking into a case that has us looking into any missing persons cases involving women around your daughter's age."

"Oh my God," Shelby said. She started to tremble and suddenly tossed the cigarette into the yard as if it had come alive and bitten her.

"There's no need to assume the worst," Ellington said.

"That's right," Mackenzie agreed. "Some of your answers could very well easily eliminate her from this case."

"Okay," Shelby said. She sat down in the rocker behind her and looked out to the street. "I tried to tell myself that I was stupid to call the police. Daisy is twenty-two years old. So what if she goes out of touch for a day or so. But…well, she was supposed to have dinner with me last night and she never showed. She never called or even texted and that is *not* like Daisy at all. I tried calling her boyfriend because I assumed that's where she was, but he's not answering his phone."

"How well do you know her boyfriend?" Mackenzie asked.

"Well enough. They've been dating for about two years. He's a good one. I feel safe in saying that he shouldn't be on your list of suspicious people at all."

"They spend a lot of time together?" Ellington asked.

"They spend *most* of their time together. They practically live together."

"Any idea if they had any plans yesterday?"

"No. Brian, her boyfriend, works from home as a freelance graphic artist. And Daisy is going to school part time while she waits tables at night. Yesterday was one of her days off and when they can arrange it, they just spend the day together. They'll go to a movie or just run errands together. That sort of thing."

"What's the boyfriend's full name?" Mackenzie asked.

"Brian Dixon."

"Can you think of anyone either of them might consider an enemy?" Mackenzie asked.

"No. I mean, I know that Brian and his brother don't get along...sort of estranged. But they never even talk. I think his brother lives out in Olympia somewhere."

"Mrs. Walker, do you happen to know if Daisy or Brian rented a storage unit anywhere in town?"

"No, neither of them do. And neither of them *need* to. Brian owns his own house, something he bought off of his parents before they moved across the country. He has this messy garage that he keeps everything in. Daisy sometimes joked to him that she's afraid to go in there because the mess will come alive and eat her."

"What kind of stuff is in there?" Ellington asked.

"Oh, I don't know. I've only seen it once or twice. Just...everything. His lawnmower, old footballs and kites, tools, boxes of old Christmas and Halloween decorations. Things like that."

"Have you happened to go by there since you felt your daughter might be missing?" Mackenzie asked.

"I drove by there, but his car wasn't there. Daisy's was, but they take his car everywhere."

"Can you give us his address?" Mackenzie asked. She figured it wouldn't hurt to look by the boyfriend's house although she was already certain that this was going to lead nowhere. She was pretty sure that if she and Ellington really dug into it, Brian and Daisy had decided to get the hell out of Seattle, away from what appeared to be a loving yet overprotective mother.

"Mrs. Walker," Ellington said, "does Daisy live with you?"

"This is her address, yes. But she's usually at Brian's house."

"I wonder if she might have a phone or a laptop she might have left here?"

"Yes, actually. Her laptop is still in her room. I know because I checked it to see if maybe she had left a note on it that might have pointed towards where she might be."

"What about a cell phone?"

"No, I assume she has that with her. I tried using the Find Friends feature on my phone—something we used to use when I hurt my knee two years ago and she kept tabs on me when I was walking around the block to rehab it. But her phone isn't picking up. I'm pretty sure it's dead."

"Would you allow us to take the laptop with us?" Ellington asked. "Maybe if we can get someone at the PD to check it out, we can figure out some more details."

"And if you'll give us her phone number," Mackenzie added, "we'll see if we can gather a location on where it might be."

"Yes, I'd be fine with all of that." She considered something for a moment and then got up from the rocker. "I'll be right back," she said as she headed inside.

"You think that's even worth looking into?" Mackenzie asked.

"I think it's worth a shot. These women…to be taken in a way that allows them to be bound and gagged without being too seriously injured before the stab wound to the chest…it makes me wonder if they are *going* to the killer. Maybe they are meeting him somewhere for some reason or another."

It was a good thought and one that she felt rather silly for missing.

Mrs. Walker came back out several seconds later, carrying Daisy's laptop. She handed it over to Ellington almost reluctantly. "Please let me know when you find her…no matter what the result is."

It pained Mackenzie to see that this mother had already assumed her daughter was dead. She wanted to reassure her but knew that she could not, merely from a professional standpoint.

"Someone will certainly be in touch as we get deeper into this," was all she said. "In the meantime, please do contact the police if you think of anything else that might be relevant to your daughter's whereabouts."

Mrs. Walker nodded as the agents took their leave. Mackenzie watched the poor lady walk back up her porch steps as she got into the car. She looked defeated—like she had already given up.

"You think it's connected?" Ellington asked as he got behind the wheel.

"I don't know. It doesn't feel right. But then again, nothing about this case has really felt right."

Ellington said nothing else. He cranked the car and pulled out into the street. She could tell that he was being choosy about what he said to her now, still walking on eggshells as a result of their earlier argument. Part of her was glad. She felt that she needed to explore the case deeper and she'd do a better job of that working in silence, without anyone else's thoughts or theories getting in her way.

We're missing something, she thought. *Maybe we're missing a few different things. Something that's right in front of us...but what?*

It gnawed at her as they headed back to the police station. It was the first time in her career that she actually started to wonder if they'd return to DC with the case still open—with a killer still on the loose and a puzzle left unsolved.

It hurt to think it, but in the gloomy afternoon that stretched out ahead of them, it seemed entirely possible.

CHAPTER TWENTY SIX

If there was ever any doubt that Ellington knew her well, it was eliminated the moment they got back to the station. He left her to her thoughts, giving her the conference room while he met up with Rising and some of the other officers to continue going down the list of local storage facilities.

With the room to herself, she took all of the records they had accumulated so far and started spreading them out on the table. When she had them in an order that made sense to her, she went to the whiteboard and started making notes. As she wrote down her notes, she began reciting facts and figures to herself, as if cramming for an exam. The thoughts streamed through her head like a flooded river, coming out through her fingers and the dry-erase marker.

When it's all said and done, the dolls are going to mean something. Even if it seems like a very small detail to the nature of the deaths themselves, the dolls and the tea stuff clearly mean something to the killer. But what? And why?

Maybe the storage units are a sign that the killer likes to hide things. Maybe it's more than just some clever way to hide bodies that he kills. Is there an inherent symbolism there or is it something psychological that he's not even aware of? Hiding things…storing them as if they were valuable, like personal belongings…something like that.

But why in storage units? Why something so public and small and…

Mackenzie paused for a moment. She stared at the board, looking at the notes she had jotted down. There was something there, something in the last thought that might be worth digging into…

She went back to the files and read over the preliminary facts and figures. She stopped at the file depicting the scene at U-Store-It. She scanned the first page and found what she was looking for.

Unit measurements, 10 x 8.

She remembered thinking how the units there had been rather small—especially considering just how large the place had been.

She then looked at the very first stack of papers that made up the file for the scene that had started this all for them: Quinn Tuck's Seattle Storage Solutions. It had been a decent-looking place but what's more, she had left there thinking the units had looked rather tiny. She looked to the details of the case and found the size: *8x8.*

She was well aware that it could mean nothing, but she was willing to grasp at even the smallest straw now. She looked back over to the file for U-Store-It and found Ralph Underwood's number. She called it up and was pleased when he answered on the second ring.

"This is U-Store-It," he answered.

"Mr. Underwood, this is Agent White with the FBI."

"Oh. Hi. Look, I've already closed the place until further notice," he said, clearly irritated. "What else do you need from me?"

"I just had some questions about storage units. I was wondering if all of your units are eight-by-eight in size."

"No. I have a few economy-sized ones. I offer several sizes, all the way up to twenty-by-sixteen."

"And what would you say the average storage unit size is?"

"Probably ten-by-fifteen. From what I've seen, most of them come in that size."

"So would the eight-by-eight units you have be considered small?"

"Yeah. They make them smaller, but not a lot of facilities carry them. They're pretty useless."

"What about other facilities in the city? Do you think most of them stick with that average size of ten-by-fifteen?"

"I'd think so. But there are a few that do like I do—offer a few different sizes."

Mackenzie thought about this for a moment, nodding to herself as a theory started to take shape.

"Do you know the smallest that are offered?"

"I'm not sure. I've seen them as small as around seven-by-five."

"Thank you, Mr. Underwood."

"Is that all?"

"For now, yes. Thanks again for your help."

She ended the call and once again went back to the files. As she found what she needed, she jotted it up on the whiteboard. As she wrote down what she needed, a knock sounded at the door. It opened slowly as Ellington walked in.

"How you doing?" he asked.

She wasn't sure if he meant in regards to the case or their little argument, so she only shrugged. "I think I might have an avenue to check out. Could be nothing, but in a case this odd and frustrating, I'm willing to try just about anything."

"What've you got? I hope it's better than my news. It does appear that we won't be able to find Daisy's phone. It's either dead or out of service."

"Yeah, mine's better."

She filled him in on the conversation she had just had with Ralph Underwood. She then tapped at the whiteboard and showed him what she was writing down when he'd entered the room.

"Every single one of the units the killer is using is smaller than average. Ten-by-eight, eight-by-eight, even an eight-by-six, which is the smallest of them all."

The flicker of excitement in his eyes made her feel confident that she had potentially stumbled onto something. "Any idea what it might mean?"

"I don't know. But everything about this case seems to be symbolic...whether the killer realizes it or not. He's using storage units to hide his victims. He's setting up bizarre little tea party scenes in a very obscure way. And he's using smaller units to do it all."

"Not trying to be a smart-ass here, but maybe it's a cost-saving technique? I'd imagine the smaller units are cheaper to rent."

"That's true but...I don't know. I think it might mean something. Maybe something to do with confinement or some personal issue. Maybe...maybe claustrophobia."

"But wouldn't he try to *avoid* small spaces if that were the case?"

"Not if he's subconsciously trying to overcome it."

Again, Ellington got that little flicker in his eyes. "So where do we start?"

"We need to call everyone all over again. I want to find the facilities outside of the ones the killer has already used that offer very small units. Anything smaller than ten-by-ten. And any that have been paid for in cash should be red-flagged."

"Anything else?" he asked.

She thought about the dolls, about the tea party items. There was something there, too. She was sure of it. Not just a meaning, but maybe an avenue for a lead. She could feel it teasing at the edges of her reasoning but she couldn't quite grasp it just yet.

"I think that's all for now," she said. "I'll find Rising and see if I can get him to assemble a team."

She headed for the door and on her way out, Ellington took her by the arm. She turned to look at him and saw that he suddenly had a very serious look in his eyes.

"Are you okay?" he asked.

"Yeah."

"Are *we* okay?"

"Yes, we're okay. We need to talk for sure, but now's not the time. Call it the work-obsessed part of me if you want, but that's the way it is."

She wished she could take back the last little barb but it was too late. She let it hang in the air between them as she headed out of the conference room.

***

Including Rising, there were four officers already calling up the owner of the storage facilities in the city and surrounding towns. With Mackenzie's new request, two others were also thrown at the task, including the department's secretary.

While she waited, Mackenzie and Ellington remained in the conference room to continue going over the files. While Mackenzie underwent a quick study of each of the victims for what felt like the hundredth time, she could feel Ellington's gaze on her from time to time. She knew that he loved her without question and felt bad for being so cold to him over the course of the last day or so. She knew it came down to her own insecurities and a fear of getting married, but there was no time to delve into all of that right now. Maybe on the way home, after they'd cracked this case.

If we crack this case at all, she thought.

She was about to leave the room and ask if there was any new information on the missing persons case regarding Daisy Walker when Rising entered the room. He had a single Post-it note in his hand, which he slapped on the desk between them.

"Twenty-six places called so far, and these are the only two not already on the killer's list that offer smaller units," he said. "One of them is about thirty miles away, on the other side of Redmond. The other is somewhere downtown...and just happens to be one of the places that has refused to shut down while we conduct the investigation. And because of his shitty attitude, he would not give a name for the unit, though he did say it was paid for in cash."

"Are there already officers on the scene?" Mackenzie asked.

"No. We're meeting up as a force in about an hour to divide up the real estate and set up shifts."

"We'll start with the one downtown, then," Mackenzie said. "Can you have someone roll by the one in Redmond just to have a look around?"

"Can do."

Mackenzie wasted no time in tidying up the table, still littered with the case files and notes. She and Ellington left the room in a hurry. As they did, Mackenzie realized that not only was she exhausted, but she was starting to feel slightly ill. She tried to remember if she'd eaten much of a breakfast and could barely remember what she'd had. This damned case…it was really getting to her. She had to settle down…had to calm herself.

Should probably see a doctor or a shrink when I get back to DC, she thought as they headed for the car. And then, on the heels of that, she returned to the horrifying hunch that had come to her earlier…one she did not want to face in light of what she and Ellington were potentially headed toward downtown.

She kept it all to herself, though she did let Ellington drive. And as she watched the city pass by, she found herself looking over to Ellington. She thought of him as a husband and realized it was something she wanted very badly. Only, now that it was so close to being a reality, it scared her.

Many things were scaring her, actually. She just hoped she was hiding it well from Ellington rather than unintentionally using that fear to push him away.

In an almost subconscious movement, Mackenzie placed her hand over her stomach as Ellington drove them toward the downtown district.

CHAPTER TWENTY SEVEN

They arrived at Roy's Storage just after three o'clock in the afternoon. It was situated in an old parking lot, fenced in by black metal slats. The neighboring businesses were a barber shop and what appeared to be an abandoned and long-neglected bakery of some kind. An auto garage sat across the street, one of the bay doors blocked off with spare tires. It wasn't quite what some might call the "bad part of town" but it was pretty close.

They pulled into the parking lot and parked in front of the main office. There were two other vehicles there. Wasting little time, they walked directly inside where they found a man—presumably Roy, the owner—sitting behind a counter with his feet kicked up. He was scrolling through Facebook on his phone. He looked up at Mackenzie and Ellington as if he were in the middle of some very important work, and set his phone down.

"Can I help you folks?" he asked.

Ellington showed his ID and did the introductions. Roy sighed and shook his head. "Did the cops actually call the feds because I refused to shut down my business?"

"Not at all," Ellington said. "However, our case has led us to believe that we may need to take a closer look at the storage facilities that offer smaller units."

"Can I ask why?"

"No," Mackenzie snapped. "We'd really just appreciate *some* cooperation from you. Can you tell us how many of your units are of a smaller size? We're looking for anything smaller than ten-by-ten."

He seemed to size her up in a way that made Mackenzie think he might consider getting rude with her if Ellington wasn't there. Roy then looked back and forth between the two of them and let out a chuckle of disbelief. He reached under the counter and grabbed a key ring that was decked out with at least thirty keys.

"The keys with the yellow heads are all for the smaller units. They're going to be the ones closest to the parking lot."

"Thanks," Ellington said, taking the keys from him. "We'll try to be as quick as possible."

They walked back outside and around the back of the office building. The storage units were basic storage sheds, situated within several feet of one another. As Roy had indicated, the smaller ones sat closest to them. They seemed to be in pretty good shape; had the location and the parking lot not seemed so grim and cheap, they would have looked almost normal in a nicer facility.

As they approached the first storage shed, marked A1, Ellington flipped through the keys until he found one with a yellow head. A strip of yellow tape ran along the top and the marking **A1** had been written on it.

Ellington unlocked the rollaway door and pushed it up. It rolled noiselessly on the rails and revealed a space that had been packed out. There was an old grill, two old bikes, several carboard boxes, milk crates stuffed with CDs and DVDs—a little bit of everything. Even if they had suspected a body to be hiding away in this unit, one glance told them that there wasn't enough room to store such a thing.

As Ellington pulled the door back down, Mackenzie caught slight movement out of the corner of her eye back toward the office building. While they had been inside, someone else had pulled up. They were driving a black Ford pickup truck and had parked directly beside their car. The driver had opened the door and was looking out their way. It looked like he had been prepared to get out of the truck and perhaps go into the office or walk to the storage sheds. But he had stopped, still standing behind the open truck door, frozen while he gazed at them.

"Ellington," she said quietly. "Look."

Ellington followed her gaze and saw the man, too. He was wearing a baseball cap, low over his brow. He pulled it a little tighter down over his brow and lowered his head as he started to get back into the truck.

"Excuse me!" Mackenzie called out. "Sir, can we ask you a few questions?"

He ignored her and closed the door. Mackenzie then looked to Ellington and they communicated without words. Ellington started walking quickly forward while Mackenzie kept a slower pace behind him.

Ellington had made it a few steps before the truck cranked to life. Ellington raise his badge and ID, yelling out, "FBI!"

The driver did not care. He backed out quickly, nearly colliding with a passing car. A blaring horn split the afternoon, causing the driver to slam on his brakes. That was the opportunity Ellington needed. He rushed forward, his hand hovering over the butt of his Glock.

Mackenzie quickened her pace, ready to jump into the car and give chase if necessary.

Ellington made it to the truck just as the car that had nearly been hit veered around the back of the truck. He grabbed at the door handle but the door was clearly locked. He knocked on the window hard; Mackenzie could tell that he was losing his cool.

As she rushed forward to help, she took note of the license plate and committed it to memory.

And that's when she heard the gunshot.

Ellington cried out and stumbled back, falling to the ground. Mackenzie's heart stopped beating for a moment as she reached for her sidearm. She pulled it right away as she took in the scene in the course of a split second.

The driver had fired a shot through the window. Glass was all over the ground, some of it covering Ellington. He was moving, going for his gun. She saw the driver reaching out of the window to fire another shot.

Mackenzie moved as if it was second nature. She raised the gun and took aim one inch to the left of the shape of the driver. She did not want to kill him, just scare him. She fired and her shot tore through the windshield in a perfect little circle.

The driver's arm went back inside and the truck sped back out into the road. The sound of screeching tires and horn sounded out as the truck spun straight into the road and then sped forward.

Mackenzie ran forward, a lump rising in her throat. *Please be okay, please be okay...* That comment raced through her head in a continuous stream as she made it to Ellington. She saw him slowly sitting up and, perhaps more importantly, saw no blood.

"Are you hit?" she asked, fighting back tears.

"No. He must have been rushed or disoriented. I was lucky as hell."

"Can you get up?"

Ellington nodded and they hurried to the car. Without any discussion, Mackenzie took the wheel. Another of their ongoing inside jokes was how Mackenzie was a much better driver than Ellington. That, coupled with the fact that he had just nearly been shot in the head, made it a no-brainer.

As they peeled out of the parking lot, Roy stepped out of the office, yelling something at them. He was clearly pissed that shots had been fired in his facility. Mackenzie ignored him and straightened out the car's course in the road. She saw the black truck up ahead, having just shot through a stoplight that was turning yellow.

Mackenzie gunned the gas and laid down on the horn. Beside her, Ellington was slowly strapping on his seatbelt. "Careful," he said.

"Always," Mackenzie replied through clenched teeth.

"You get the asshole's license plate number?" he asked.

"I did. Can you call Rising?"

As Ellington pulled out his phone, Mackenzie tore through the stoplight, now red. Her horn had alerted everyone who was coming up to the light, but she still had to swerve hard to the left to keep from hitting another car. She straightened the car out just in time to see the truck take a right turn at the end of the block. The back end of it jumped up on the sidewalk, nearly taking out a pedestrian.

While Mackenzie sped to the same turn, Ellington had gotten Rising on the phone. Mackenzie focused on his end of the conversation while she drove, wanting to be on top of everything without having him repeat it to her while she tried to chase down the man in the truck—a man she was assuming was their killer.

"Rising, we're in pursuit of a black Ford truck that just turned on Wythe Street. The driver took a shot at me when we tried to stop him at Roy's Storage. I need you to get units out here to help right now. License plate on the truck is…"

Mackenzie recited the number loudly as she took the turn. The truck, meanwhile, had somehow increased its lead. It was about fifty yards ahead of them now. As she sped after it, the truck barreled through a red light, bringing lines of traffic on both sides to a shuddering halt. One car was rear-ended and another came very close to slamming into a dump truck.

Mackenzie laid down on the horn, knowing that the longer this chase went on, the chances of a serious accident occurring increased. She also went through the red light. Up ahead, the black truck took another turn. Mackenzie punched the gas to the floor. The car surged forward and gained some ground. When she took the same turn, the truck was now about thirty yards away.

She watched as it went through a stoplight—a green one for once. Yet as it crossed through and Mackenzie approached, it turned yellow. Mackenzie continued to lay down on the horn but it did not seem to register with the driver of the red van that was coming in from the right. As the light turned red in front of Mackenzie, it tuned green for the van reaching the intersection. It started creeping through, moving at a pace that would put it directly in front of Mackenzie.

"Stop!" Mackenzie screamed.

Of course, the driver did not hear her.

She had no choice but to slam on brakes as the van made it cross the intersection. Still blasting the horn, Mackenzie started up again, heading through the intersection. When she cleared it, she saw a straight stretch of road with a few cars coming and going. But she did not see the black truck anywhere.

"Damn it," Mackenzie said.

"It's okay," Ellington said. "That was a bad-ass bit of driving." He then pulled out his phone and called up Rising again. Within a few seconds, he was reporting to the deputy. "We lost him just after the intersection at Nelson and Fifth. See if you can set up some sort of perimeter, would you?"

He ended the call as Mackenzie pulled a quick U-turn at the next intersection.

"Heading back to Roy's Storage?" Ellington asked.

"Absolutely. I want to see what this guy was afraid for us to see."

"You thinking he's the killer, too?"

"If he's not *our* killer, he's certainly some type of killer. Shit...Ellington, are you okay?"

"Yeah. The adrenaline is still fresh."

"Did you get a good look at him?"

"No. Just the jawline and mouth. He was smart. He never once looked at me, not even when he was reaching out of the window to kill me. Nice shooting on your part, by the way. You saved my life, you know."

"Glad to do it," she said. It was a generic comment, but it was all that she could manage in that moment, as she felt like she might be on the verge of crying. "Now let's go see what this asshole was hiding."

CHAPTER TWENTY EIGHT

By the time they returned to the unit, the Seattle police were in pursuit of the black Ford pickup truck. This time, Mackenzie went past the main office and the parking lot, straight for the paved aisle between the storage sheds. She checked her rearview and saw Roy, the owner, come rushing out of the office after them.

Mackenzie parked the car halfway down the aisle and got out. Ellington joined her, taking out the key ring Roy had given them earlier. Mackenzie wondered if that was the source of his irritation—that they quickly left the property with all of his spare keys.

"What the hell happened?" Roy asked as he met up with them. He was red in the face with worry and anger. Part of Mackenzie almost *hoped* he'd say something out of line so she could set him straight.

"One of your clients took a shot at me is what happened," Ellington said. "Good thing he was in a hurry to get away, too, or you'd have my brains on your pavement."

"You got a call earlier today from the police, asking about the size of some your units, correct?" Mackenzie asked.

"Yeah…asking about small-sized ones."

"We're looking for a murderer," Mackenzie said. "And we have reason to believe he is using storage sheds—small ones."

"Using them for what?"

Mackenzie shook her head. She wasn't about to tell this guy all of the details. "Please…just let us do our jobs. You told the cops on the phone that you had smaller units and that some of them were paid in cash, right?"

"Well, just two of them."

"Is one of them rented by a man named Mark Riley?"

Sensing that he was truly in the hot seat, Roy put his hands on his hips and looked behind the agents, toward the sheds. "Yeah. Unit 4B."

"Thanks," Mackenzie said, already turning to head in the direction of the sheds.

"Do I need to be worried here?" Roy asked, clearly scared now.

I wish I knew, Mackenzie thought as she and Ellington ran to Unit 4B. She had to give it to Ellington—for nearly being shot in the face less than fifteen minutes ago, he sure had his wits about him. Maybe he was more determined now, pushing forward with something of a personal vendetta.

At 4B, they came to a stop and Ellington inserted the key into the lock. The lock was built directly into the side of the sliding door and when he turned it, the door seemed to give a bit. As he pushed the door up along its tracks, Mackenzie withdrew her Glock. She knew it was a silly thing to do; if there was *anything* in there, it was likely a dead body. Still, after what they'd experienced this afternoon, she wasn't about to take any chances.

The door rolled up, revealing a mostly empty unit. In the back, there were two overturned carboard boxes. Inside one of them were the shattered fragments of something porcelain. Likely a teapot.

But tucked away in the far corner was a small tackle box, the kind a beginning fisherman might take out on the river or a pond. Ellington walked slowly toward it, looking back to Mackenzie as if to tell her that it was okay—that he was going to be careful. He hunkered down to his knees and unclasped the top. When he opened it, he got to his feet and stepped back.

"Damn," he said.

Mackenzie joined him and looked inside the tacklebox. Inside, there were three knives. One had very clearly been used, the blade coated in dried blood with splatters on the handle.

"I think it's safe to say this is one of his," Ellington said.

"But the question is whether or not he intended to put a body in it," Mackenzie said.

They both looked around the area, trying to imagine a dead body on the floor. They'd seen it enough times over the last few days that it wasn't all that easy to picture.

"Hell," Ellington said, "there's no way to know for sure. We know that he's not above storing the bodies in the storage units of his victims. He's done it once. There's no rhyme or reason to it, no—"

The ringing of his phone interrupted his thought. He answered it quickly, still looking around the unit like a potential customer might survey it.

"This is Ellington."

Mackenzie listened to his end of the conversation, though it was mainly just a series of *yeahs* and *okays.* She looked at the empty boxes, their presence making her think that at some time, there had been something else here. Maybe the killer had once had many of his dolls and tea items here. Maybe he constantly moved them from one unit to another just in case he was ever caught or slipped up. It was a smart play on his part but in this case, it might very well be a big mistake on his part.

At least, that's what she hoped.

Ellington ended the call and already had a look of deep thought on his face. "That was Rising. They found the truck, but the driver was missing. It was about two miles away from where we lost it, crashed into a utility pole."

"No sign of the driver at all?"

"No. But they ran the plate. The truck belonged to someone named Brian Dixon. I don't know why, but that name sounds very familiar."

In Mackenzie's head, something clicked. Finally, some progress…

"That's the boyfriend of the missing persons case—of Daisy Walker."

"That's right!" He looked like he had just remembered the lyrics to some long forgotten song, the words finally surfacing in his head. "But…wait. Dixon is the killer?"

"I doubt it. No…I don't think so. That doesn't feel right."

"It seems like the simplest solution right now," he said. "Daisy Walker is reported missing by her mother. A mother who openly admits that her daughter spends all of her time with her boyfriend. A truck belonging to that boyfriend pulls into a storage facility we just happen to be looking into and then the driver tries to blow my head off. If he's the killer, maybe he killed his girlfriend, too. Maybe he killed Daisy."

But even as he spoke all of it out loud, Mackenzie could tell that he was even starting to see it as not making much sense.

"All we would need to do is dust the truck for prints," Mackenzie said. "This unit, too. A thorough search of Dixon's house would also probably pull up some sort of documentation for at least one of the units. That's *if* he's the killer. Which I doubt."

"Rising said he'll have forensics out here in about half an hour for prints."

"Once they get here, I say we check Dixon's house. Just in case."

"And then we join in on the manhunt for the driver of the truck."

"Based on what, exactly? Your description of the hat he was wearing and the angle of his jawline? I hate to say it, but unless he was injured when he crashed into that utility pole, he's gotten away."

"Yeah, probably…"

"So instead of looking for *him,* we need to find more information. I do think that the killer driving the truck belonging to Daisy Walker's boyfriend all but confirms that she's the next victim. So between Daisy, the truck, this unit, and everything we already have, we should finally be able to move ahead. Maybe find out where he would be if he had to go into hiding."

"If he hasn't already made a plan to leave town when the shit hits the fan," Ellington added.

"We can't afford to think like that," Mackenzie said.

"I know. It's just frustrating the hell out of me."

"Me, too."

But for Mackenzie, it was more than that. Knowing there was a woman out there, perhaps still alive, perhaps not even given that death sentence of a stab wound yet, was maddening. All they needed was one more little push in the right direction and they might be able to potentially save her.

And in her mind's eye, she saw that woman—presumably Daisy Walker—lying on a cold concrete floor with a gag around her mouth, her legs and feet tied tightly. She was squirming and looking to the back of the storage door, wondering if anyone was going to help her.

And really, she was nothing more than one of those lifeless dolls that had been taunting them, all glassy eyes and little hopeless stares.

CHAPTER TWENTY NINE

The afternoon went by in a rainy blur. Forensics showed up at Roy's Storage and started going through their process. Mackenzie and Ellington took their leave and headed back to Shelby Walker's house. It was not a visit that Mackenzie wanted to make. They'd all but be confirming that her daughter might very well indeed be in serious danger—danger that could very well lead to death.

Mackenzie attempted to call before stopping by but Shelby was not answering her phone. Several horrible scenarios ran through her head but she did her best to keep them in check. This case had been terrible for her as far as keeping herself in check. And now that there was a mother's heart and possibly even sanity on the line, she had to remain professional.

They arrived at Shelby Walker's house at 6:12 p.m. Mackenzie was incredibly saddened to see that Mrs. Walker was still sitting on the porch in just about the same place and posture as she had been that morning. When she saw the car pull up alongside the curb, she stood up and her hand went to her mouth as if to push down a scream.

The moment Mackenzie was out of the car, she did her best to calm her. "It's not what it might seem like," Mackenzie said. "We just have a few more questions and maybe some information that might help."

Mrs. Walker seemed very skeptical, eyeing the agents like they might attack her if they came up on her porch. Still, she nodded to the stairs in an invitation, slowly resuming her seated position.

"What information?" she asked.

"Earlier today, you told us that Daisy and her boyfriend, Brian Dixon, spent a lot of time together. You also indicated that they usually took Brian's car everywhere. But do you happen to know whether or not he also owns a truck?"

"He does, but it this old beater truck. He rarely drives it. Hauls the trash off in it, helps people move, things like that."

"Is it a black Ford?" Ellington asked.

"I…I think so. Why? What is it? What's happened?"

"Well, it was involved in a police chase earlier today. We don't believe Brian was at the wheel. We think the truck might have been stolen."

"By who?"

"We aren't sure yet. But we do have reason to believe it might have been stolen by a suspect in a murder case."

Mrs. Walker's reaction was just about what Mackenzie had expected. Her mouth seemed to contort as she let out a gnashing cry. Her eyes watered as her hand once again went to her mouth in the universal sign of grief.

"Now, please keep in mind...we don't have enough hard evidence to confirm any of this. But we do know that Brian's car was indeed involved in a chase and accident earlier today. But the driver was not in the truck when it crashed."

"Oh…"

This seemed to ease her a bit, making her relax the slightest little bit. "I can tell you with some assurance that Brian is not the type to lead the police on a chase." She took a gulp of air here, as if she was not quite sure she wanted to bail on her grief and negative thoughts just yet. "I don't think he's ever been in any kind of trouble, aside from some parking tickets."

"Did he always keep the truck at his home?" Mackenzie asked.

"Oh, I don't know for sure. I saw it in front of his garage once. I figured that's where he kept it because the garage was always so crammed and messy."

"And you can't think of *anywhere* the two of them might have gone?"

"Not without Daisy telling me," Mrs. Walker said.

"Okay. Thank you again for your time."

"Wait…Agents…do you think this murderer got my Daisy?"

Mackenzie hated such direct questions. She wasn't opposed to stretching the truth to help ease someone's mind when it was necessary, but she hated to lie. So she did the best with what she had at the time.

"It's just too early to say. For now, I think the fact that she turned up missing *with* her boyfriend is a good sign. There's certainly no need to give up hope."

Once again, she saw Mrs. Walker relax a bit more. Still, a single tear escaped the corner of her eye and Mackenzie could tell that the poor old woman had already spent much of the day assuming the absolute worst.

"Do you think you'll find her?" Mrs. Walker asked.

Again, not wanting to tell an outright lie, Mackenzie did the best she could. "We're certainly going to try our best."

It sounded like defeat. She hoped Mrs. Walker couldn't hear it and didn't take the chance to look back at her face as she and

Ellington headed back to the car, leaving Shelby Walker with more questions than answers for the second time that day.

***

They spent the next hour going through Brian Dixon's house. It was a simple yet quaint one-story house located three miles away from Shelby Walker's house. It showed the signs of cohabitation—clearly from a couple close to one another but not yet married. The shampoos and soaps were all mixed up together in the shower. The books and DVDs in the living room were incredibly varied and not hidden out of sight. Daisy's comb was on the bedside table on the left side of the bed while a MacBook sat charging on the right.

What the house did not offer them was any indication that Brian Dixon had ever rented a storage unit. Even when Ellington picked open the lock on a lower drawer to a filing cabinet in Brian's office, there was nothing. There was, however, a brochure for wedding rings. Seeing that Brian had circled two in red marker made Mackenzie sadder than it should have.

The last place they checked was the garage. Shelby Walker had not been kidding; the garage was a mitigated disaster. There was a little bit of everything, some of which made no sense at all: sports equipment, a portion of a department store mannequin, a small collection of glass bottles, old stereo equipment, and boxes of decorations for every holiday, right down to St. Patrick's Day.

"I think it's safe to say that if anyone *needed* a storage unit, it would be this guy," Ellington said.

"But I think the fact that his garage is such a mess shows that he doesn't. Not to mention that there was no sign of it inside."

"So Brian Dixon is not our killer. Which means his truck was indeed stolen—more than likely by our killer."

"That's what it looks like."

"We need to get back to the station and see what forensics is up to. If they can get just once clear print from the truck or the unit…"

"Yeah, it won't hurt to hope," Mackenzie said.

They exited the house as dusk darkened into night. On the way to the car, Mackenzie found herself reaching out and taking Ellington's hand. She gave it a squeeze and smiled thinly at him.

"I'm glad you didn't die today," she said.

"Yeah, me too. I won't lie…I thought I had pissed myself there for a second."

She wanted to try to express to him just how worried she had been when she'd heard the shot and seen him go down. For a moment there, she was sure she had lost him and her heart had not been able to understand it—to comprehend it. But to admit such a thing meant showing vulnerability. And this close to the wedding—not to mention on the heels of a fight—she did not want to put herself in that position.

They pulled away from Brian Dixon's home and as Mackenzie looked back at the house in the rearview mirror, she was overcome with a certainty that chilled her. Maybe it was a woman's intuition or the instinctual extra sense she was developing as an agent. Whatever it was, the night seemed to fill her in, making her all but certain that Brian Dixon was never going to step foot in his house again and that Daisy Walker was in for some serious trouble…if she wasn't already dead.

CHAPTER THIRTY

Back at the station, the atmosphere had a tension that made Mackenzie feel like there was a bomb somewhere in the building and it might go off at any moment. In addition to the storage unit killer, there were also several cops tied up in a heroin bust that was going down later that night. Word of Ellington's near-death experience had made the rounds and most of the officers in the building were looking at him with something close to reverence.

When they entered the conference room, Rising was there with the two officers who had assisted him the previous day: Dentry and Willard. Dentry was on the phone, huddled in the corner of the room. Based on the bits of conversation Mackenzie was picking up, she was speaking to someone with forensics.

"Any luck on your end?" Rising asked them as they entered.

"Nothing," Ellington said. "Though we feel pretty confident that we can eliminate Brian Dixon as the killer. There's nothing at all in his house that indicates he has anything to do with the murders. No record of storage rentals, no red flags at home…nothing."

"His packed-out garage also hints at the fact that he has never even thought of using a storage unit," Mackenzie added.

"So the truck was stolen?" Rising asked.

"That's what we're thinking."

They then filled Rising in on the conversation they'd had with Shelby Walker and their search of Dixon's home. When they informed him that Brian Dixon was Daisy Walker's boyfriend, a look of understanding flashed across Rising's face.

"So chances are pretty good that Walker is the next victim," he said.

"That's our theory," Mackenzie agreed.

"What about Dixon? You think he was killed just out of sheer poor luck? I mean, the killer had to get the truck somehow."

"That's just another question we're going to have to find an answer to," Ellington said.

The three of them stood around the table, allowing a brief silence to hang around them as they let this all sink in. The silence was short-lived, however. Dentry ended her call and turned to them slowly. The look on her face indicated that any news she had was not going to be good.

"That was Rodgers, with forensics," Dentry said. "There were no prints in the storage unit."

"Not a single one?" Rising asked.

"That's what they're saying. There was a fraction of one on one of the cardboard boxes, but it's so poor, they don't think they can get a reading from it."

"What about the truck?" Mackenzie asked.

"There were several prints in the truck. But based on the cleanliness of the unit, just about everyone on the scene is expecting those prints to come back as belonging to Brian Dixon."

"How long before we'll have results?"

"Early morning," Dentry said.

"And please understand," Rising said. "With this whole heroin bust and then the units out in patrol, we can't really offer much more manpower on this."

"We may need to consider calling DC and getting a few more agents on this," Ellington said. "Maybe get an agent or two from the Seattle field office."

"That's not a bad idea," Rising said.

"I'll make the call to McGrath," Ellington said.

The look he gave Mackenzie was one that looked very close to defeat. Calling McGrath would mean admitting that this case had been a little too much for them...this, their last case together as a couple. She nearly argued against him making the call; if there wasn't a life hanging in the balance, she might have done it. But right now, she could put her own ego on hold. Right now, locating either the killer or Daisy Walker was the most important thing.

Ellington stepped out of the office, leaving Mackenzie with Rising and his pair of assisting officers. She looked at the mess on the table—files, printouts, crime scene photographs. She then looked at the whiteboard, at all of the notes and scribbles that had been jotted down over the last few days.

It all has to mean something, right? she thought. *This has to have an ending somewhere. In all of these notes and folders, there's an answer. I just have to find it.*

But then there was another thought, one that started clanging like an old rusty cymbal in her head.

But what if you don't yet have all of the information? What if there's something else left to find?

It was that thought, nagging like an insect around her head, that sent her walking out of the conference room. She had missed something, had overlooked something. Maybe it was because of the argument with Ellington or maybe it was the fact that this case was, for some reason she still could not identify, getting under her skin. Or maybe she was too preoccupied with the wedding or the strange way she had been feeling ever since they'd landed in Seattle.

There were a myriad of reasons that could be causing her to overlook things, but at the end of the day they were all just excuses. And she was better than that. She always had been.

What's missing? What did we not see?

"You okay?"

She was barely aware that she had been wandering the hallways, lost in her own thoughts. The voice was Ellington's approaching from behind.

"Yeah," she said. "Just thinking. What did McGrath say?"

"He asked what the additional agents would be tasked with. I told him helping the local PD with the manhunt for the killer and the search for Brian Dixon and Daisy Walker, as well as any crime scene investigation. Because we have very little description of the man driving the truck, he was hesitant to give in. But he's calling the Seattle field office in a bit. He thinks we can get some assistance as early as tomorrow morning."

"Better than nothing, I guess."

"Exactly." He paused and then made a point to look directly into her eyes. "Mac...really. What's going on?"

"I don't know. I think I'm just tired. *Really* tired. And stressed out. Th wedding, this case, your mother, our fight, it's just...too much all at once. And I *loathe* that our personal crap is interfering with work."

"I get it," he said. "I really do. Look...it's already after nine. Why don't you go back to the hotel and get to bed early. Based on what Dentry said about the forensics results, we're going to probably have an early morning."

She'd usually argue against such a notion but she knew it made sense. All she could do here was go over files she'd already read through a dozen times while waiting for any calls that might come in from the cops out on the street, actively looking for any signs of a killer or the missing couple.

"I think I'll do that," she said. "Same goes for you, though. Don't stay here too long. Tomorrow's going to be a long one. Just promise that you'll call if anything new comes in."

Ellington looked up and down the hall quickly and then, seeing that the coast was clear, kissed her on the forehead. "I won't be too long. Go on and get some sleep."

He gently nudged her toward the end of the hall, toward the lobby. He gave her a wave and then headed back to the conference room. Mackenzie watched him go for only a moment before heading for the lobby.

***

Mackenzie usually had trouble falling asleep any time before eleven but that was not the case tonight. She brushed her teeth, stripped completely naked, and climbed into bed. Thoughts of the case tried to keep her awake but the pull of sleep was much stronger. She was asleep five minutes after pulling her covers around her, less than forty-five minutes after she had parted ways with Ellington in the hallway of the Seattle PD.

While asleep, she dreamed. This was nothing new, as she had been plagued with bad dreams from a young age. Those bad dreams seemed to no longer be solely about her father anymore. Those had come to a slow end after she had finally wrapped his case and had managed to move in with her life.

Still, from time to time she would experience one that reflected some trauma or another, whether from her past or the present.

The dream that rolled through her head like a tsunami that night in Seattle was no different.

While her father rarely made an appearance, those damned cornfields somehow still played a part more often than not. It was as if the stalks and husks had somehow threaded themselves into her subconscious. The Scarecrow Killer and memories associated with him rarely showed up, so that was good. But as her dream self walked through the rows, she knew that meant that her dreams were still no longer her own.

In the dream, she walked out of a cornfield, husks and corn silk in her hair and her shirt. The field came to an end at an open dirt lot. A single storage shed stood there, slightly lopsided and dirty. Overhead, the sky was slate gray, indicating a storm was on the way.

She walked toward the storage unit and found the door already open. There was nothing inside. No boxes, no bins, not even any cobwebs or mounds of dust. It was absolutely void of anything.

Yet when she stepped inside, all of that changed. She was not standing inside a dingy storage unit, but a house. It was not a house that she had ever been in before. It was just an old generic abandoned house. The walls were chipped and cracked. The furniture was old, dusty, and neglected. As she passed through the living room, she saw Deputy Rising sitting on the moldy couch. He smiled at her and pointed to the right. She looked that way and saw a hallway. It seemed to go on forever, so deep and long that it ended in a singular point of darkness, like looking down a long tunnel.

She started down the hallway and found it populated with what looked to be hundreds of doors. They were all closed and each seemed to hide its own secret. She opened one and found a dead woman on the floor, her head removed. The next revealed a rat roughly the size of a tiger, burrowing into the wall.

The next door she came to was locked. She could not open it. This was just as well because there was a woman screaming behind it. She was screaming in terror and pain. Mackenzie was somehow certain these were the cries of her mother. She walked quickly away from this door and came to the next one.

This one opened freely under her hand. She stepped into a room that she had been in recently. It was the back room in the house they had assumed belonged to the killer. The boxes and boxes of tea items and dolls had been spilled over. Some of the dolls were scattered on the floor. Something wet and sticky came out of them, something like blood but far more exaggerated.

When she looked down, Mackenzie saw that she had stepped in the stickiness. It was on her feet and somehow crawling up her ankle, twirling itself around her legs.

She cried out and stepped backward. When she did, every single doll on the floor rolled over and stared at her. They were all smiling. One was even laughing in that creepy robotic way that some dolls were capable of.

She slammed the door closed and found herself back in the hallway. She went to the next door and opened it. The room on the other side was empty with the exception of a single item.

A bassinet sat in the center of the room. It was overflowing with that same sticky stuff that had been coming off of the dolls. Mackenzie let out a little moan as she watched a small pink arm reach up out of it.

She fell back into the hall and was caught by familiar arms. She looked up and saw that Ellington was there with her. He tried to draw her close but she fought to get away when she got a good look at his face.

He was looking down at her with a set of glass eyes, plucked straight from one of the dolls in the room a bit farther back. The glassy stare seemed to cut right into her and when he pulled her close to him, his embrace was plastic. He smiled at her and that sticky stuff came out of his mouth.

"Oh, you're safe now," he said. "It's okay. You're safe. You're…"

***

"...safe. You're okay."

Mackenzie snapped awake with a gasping breath. She was in the motel room and Ellington was beside her. His hand was on her shoulder and the look of concern on his face made her slightly embarrassed.

Her heart hammered in her chest and she could not keep her legs from trembling. She looked around the room, blinking in an attempt to convince herself that she was awake...to get the dream out of her head.

"Another bad one?" he asked.

She only nodded. She then looked to the bedside clock and saw that it was 12:25. "When did you get in?" she asked.

"Eleven. I think I had just drifted off to sleep when you started moaning in your sleep. You need to talk about it?"

"God no."

She lay back down, feeling sleep already rushing back at her. She could not remember the last time she had felt this tired.

Only this time, despite the pull of sleep, she was not able to fall asleep so quickly. Remnants of the dream littered her mind. She wasn't scared, but the dream had truly done a number on her. When she realized she felt out of whack, she moved her foot under the covers and ran it along Ellington's ankle and calf. This was a sign she had used often in their relationship—a sign that she was having trouble sleeping and needed to be held. It was much easier than coming out and asking for it and Mackenzie White had never been the kind of woman who would make requests like *"I need to be held"* or *"I want to snuggle."*

Ellington sleepily obliged. He rolled over and put his arm around her. She was amazed at just how quickly she felt comforted by his touch. It was more than his arm around her. It was the pressure of his chest against her back, the mere presence of him in the bed beside her. She breathed deeply, enjoying the feeling of it.

She interlaced her fingers with the hand that had come around her side and now rested just below her breasts. He gave her hand a squeeze, still half asleep, and Mackenzie drifted away. She came in and out of sleep for the next half an hour or so, still seeing that bassinet and the sticky stuff from the dolls. She pressed herself closer into Ellington and he tightened his arm a bit.

It was a gesture of security for both of them and nothing more. But there were certain parts of their anatomy that did not understand this. She started to feel him stirring below the waist as his body responded in a very natural way to his naked fiancée so tightly pressed against him. She responded by kissing his wrist and lightly pressing her lips to his fingers, still clasped through hers. She pressed her backside against him and he slowly began kissing her on the back of the neck.

Their bodies reacted the way they usually did in those sleepy hours between midnight and five when one of their minds just wouldn't shut off. Mackenzie raised her hips slightly and reached her arm back to help guide him. When he entered her from behind, it made her feel just as secure as when he had put an arm around her.

Her back to his chest, they made love in slow yet urgent strides. It was one of the more intimate times in quite a while. When she arched her back as she reached her climax and stretched her arm back to caress the side of his face, he whispered *"I love you,"* into her ear.

And it was that statement that finally followed her down into a restful sleep, obliterating any remaining images from her horrifying dream.

CHAPTER THIRTY ONE

When the alarm of Mackenzie's phone woke her up at six in the morning, her first reaction was one of disappointment. She had fully expected to get a call from forensics or Rising with some kind of an update. Having slept through until six without being awakened by the phone also meant that there had been no significant breakthroughs during the course of the night.

When she got out of bed feeling rested and sexually satisfied from the night, she felt almost guilty. She checked her phone for any texts or emails, but found none. As she rolled out of bed, Ellington came out of the bathroom, freshly showered.

"How do you feel this morning?" he asked.

"Much better," she said.

It was mostly true. She felt well rested and the spontaneous intimate sex had been fantastic. But something still felt off. She felt a little sore, like she'd just run a small marathon, and something was out of whack with her stomach. But all in all, it was mostly minor. She could push through it and be back to normal after a shower.

As she dug out clothes from her suitcase in preparation for her shower, her phone rang. She answered it and was excited to hear Rising's voice on the other end.

"I'm afraid there's no news," he said. "Still no word from forensics on that truck, though we expect to hear something soon."

"Any news on the agents coming along from the Seattle field office?"

"Not yet. How about the two of you? What are your plans for the morning?"

"Not sure yet. I feel like it might do some good to revisit Roy's Storage. Or maybe see if there's anything we can do to help speed forensics along. There are a few other things, but I need to iron them out. We'll see you soon, one way or the other."

Rising seemed happy enough with that when they ended the call. As Mackenzie headed for the shower, still naked from the night before, Ellington started to get dressed.

"You told Rising there were a few other things," he pointed out. "Like what?"

"I think I want to go back to the house—to the killer's house. Maybe we missed something there."

"Don't you think we'd be of more use with Rising, forensics, and these new agents?"

"Certainly. Maybe the house is just something I'll check out. You head to the PD and I'll go over to the house. We'll meet up in a few hours."

"You sure?" he asked.

"Yeah. It's been nagging at me since yesterday afternoon. I want to just run one more circuit around the place."

"Okay. Just want to drop me off at the station on your way out?"

She nodded and went into the bathroom for her shower. She thought about the house and the boxes of tea party items and dolls. Images from last night's dream came rushing back, particularly the bassinet, flooded with that sticky residue.

It was an image that made her uneasy, reminding her that there was one other thing she had to do outside of the case. And she was going to have to get it done today before it drove her crazy. She sped up her shower, scrubbing a little harder as if to wash away the memories of last night's dream.

**

The house looked no less sinister in the daylight. Mackenzie arrived at 7:40, and while the sunlight coming in over the trees was quite pretty, the house seemed like one of those cliché stand-ins for a haunted house in a horror movie.

She gave the doghouse only a passing glance. The dolls inside were still having their own little eternal tea party.

Mackenzie made her way up the porch, realizing there was no guarantee that the killer wasn't here. Granted, there was no car in the sorry excuse for a driveway, but that meant nothing. After all, he had apparently stolen a truck so he might currently be without transportation of any kind.

She brought her right forearm a little closer to her holstered Glock as she opened the front door and stepped inside. She walked into the living room slowly, feeling very much like a trespasser. The place was eerily quiet—so quiet that she could hear the buzzing of an insect somewhere within the house. She stood still for a moment, just taking in the sight of the place. Everything looked untouched since the previous visit, leading her to believe that if this was indeed the killer's house, he had not been here for several days.

She wasted no time. She knew where she needed to go and did her best to convince herself that she was not uneasy. She'd seen

131

characteristics of the unstable and unhinged several times in the course of her career, but this killer was getting to her like no other. Just thinking about the several boxes of dolls and discarded children's dishes in the back room made her feel cold.

She wished Ellington was with her. She hated to feel like a scared little girl, but there it was, plain and simple. *Chalk it up as just another way this case has emotionally wrecked me.*

This thought brought to mind something else…the other task she needed to take care of but continued to put off.

The case first, she thought.

She walked down the hallway and into the back room. The boxes, for a moment, looked as if they had been subtly slithering against the back wall. She fully expected to see that blood-like fluid from her dream come spilling out of them, cascading across the floor and coming for her legs. But as the shadows cast by the sunlight stopped with her own movement, the room was, of course, not alive. It was still and neglected.

She went to the boxes and started to look through them. This time, she was not rushed. She took her time, meticulously looking through each one.

There was an assortment of items. Some of the dishes were cheap plastic discs that could be picked up at just about any dollar store in the country. But then some of them were made of some type of very delicate porcelain. Some had chips and cracks while others looked pristine. The first two boxes were filled with things like that—teapots, tea cups, plates, and even a bag filled with plastic silverware and colorful cheap cutlery designed for use in a child's play kitchen.

When she opened up the first box full of dolls, a chill rode up her spine. For a moment, she felt dizzy. She forged ahead, digging into the box and pulling out one doll after another. There was no rhyme or reason to them; some were newer and looked rather beautiful while others were clearly old and discarded, clearly leftovers from rummage sales.

As she reached the bottom of the first box of dolls, two seemingly small things happened. First, the idea of rummage sales sparked a vague notion in her head. Second, before she could catch that thought, she saw the small white smudge on the bottom of a doll's foot. She looked at the smudge and saw that it looked to be some sort of paper, only it was sticky at the edges. She scraped at it with her fingernail and it came off rather easily, rolling up as if it were a sticker.

She then thought of her rummage sale notion. *A sticker or some sort of a price tag.*

Quickly, she went back over every doll she had just taken out of the box. The first one she came to was one of the nicer ones. It was not an expensive doll by any means but its owner had taken care of it. Located on the back of its neck was the smallest little speck of white. It was surrounded by a kind of dirty hue, from where something sticky had once been—a price tag, presumably.

Some of the older dolls didn't have any indication that there had once been a price tag on their bodies. But three dolls later, she found another sticky spot on a doll's foot. Going back through the one box of dolls, she found nine that had some indication that they had once been stuck with a price tag or sticker.

She then checked the play dishes. And there, on the very first dish she looked over—a green plastic plate with scuff marks on it— she found about a quarter portion of an old sticker. It had been torn and was slightly faded but there was enough surviving print for Mackenzie to make out what it said: **DISH SET: $2**

At the very top, there was what looked like a letter, torn through. A T or an F, perhaps. And it was written in faded red, printed off of some kind of cheap printer from the looks of it.

With a new notion in mind, Mackenzie tore through the remaining boxes. She was hoping to strike pay dirt and find a sticker that had been unblemished, perhaps even with the name of a store. She knew, of course, that even then it would be difficult to nail down a single buyer, especially with an item as uninteresting as plastic dishes for a child's playset.

Twenty minutes later, with the boxes thoroughly rummaged through, she had found nearly twenty more dolls with at least some small sign that there had once been a price sticker on them. She even saw two more with that red lettering, but it was only the tops of a few letters, so it was impossible to tell what it said. A business name, she assumed.

She sat on the floor around the stacks of dolls and dishes, tea cups and pots, and thought about the next approach.

If there were stickers with a price on them, that means these weren't purchased from a store. No, these were purchased secondhand or at something like a yard sale or rummage sale. Or maybe even a secondhand thrift shop.

She found the green dish with the portion of a sticker on it and took a picture of it with her phone. She then got to her feet and fought every impulse within her to clean it up. She knew that the discovery of the stickers and the old sticker residue might mean nothing. But she had a hunch and for the first time, she was excited about a lead on this damned case.

She left the house with that excitement spurring her on. On the way to her car, she felt herself growing dizzy again. She got into the car and sat there for a moment, looking out at the house and waiting for the dizziness to pass. It subsided slowly, but not before making her feel slightly sick to her stomach.

She had a lead. One that she thought might actually be promising. But first, she had to take care of something. And knowing that it had to be the next thing on her agenda made her a little more uneasy than she had felt stepping back into that house.

***

Fifteen minutes later, she stopped by the first convenience store she could find. She knew there was a Target another fifteen minutes up the road but now that she had it in her head that she was going to finally go ahead and do this, she didn't see the sense in waiting.

She grabbed a Diet Coke and a pack of gum, feeling stupid because all she was doing was putting off why she was really there.

She located the aisle that held the little rack with travel-sized medicines and hygiene products. She looked past these, as well as the condoms located beside them. On the other side of this rack, she saw what she had come here for.

With a knot in her stomach and a flush in her cheeks, Mackenzie reached out and grabbed the first pregnancy test her hand fell on.

CHAPTER THIRTY TWO

An hour later, she was back in the conference room with Ellington. He shared with her all that he had learned while in the department that morning. Sadly, it was pretty much nothing. The agents from the Seattle field office were officially on the job now. Their first task had been investigating the unit at Roy's Storage. Unsurprisingly, they had also come up with nothing—a perfect accompaniment to the fact that the forensics team had also not found a single print.

The most recent news was that forensics had submitted their report on the Ford truck forty minutes ago. Two different sets of prints had been found. A few prints were a bit older—maybe a few weeks—and belonged to Daisy Walker. The majority of the prints, though, belonged to Brian Dixon.

"So in other words," Ellington said, slouched over the conference room table with a cup of coffee between his hands, "we got nothing out of all of this except almost catching a bullet in the face and a spirited high speed car chase."

"Well, I think I might have found something," Mackenzie said. She pulled up the picture she had taken on her phone and slid it over to Ellington.

"What am I looking at?" he asked.

"I think it's part of a sticker that thrift stores and flea markets use to place prices on their items. I'm pretty sure that one once read *Dish set, two dollars.* And then there's that red portion of a letter…"

"You think he's buying them in bulk from some place in town?"

"I think it's a possibility. And with that sticker, we should be able to narrow it down to within just a few places. Maybe even just one. I want to get some local resources on it, if we can. The local PD is going to know local businesses a hell of a lot better than either of us."

"It's the best lead we've had since getting clocked in the head," Ellington said with a lazy smile. "I think Rising can lend an officer to make the calls."

As if summoned by the very idea itself, Rising knocked on the open door and poked his head inside. "Wanted you to know that all but three storage facilities in the area are now closed until further notice. The three that were stubborn currently have a police car sitting in their parking lots for surveillance. In other words, this killer won't be able to use any more storage units."

"That's great news," Mackenzie said.

"Also, our tech guys are done with Daisy Walker's computer. There was nothing useful on there, except—we do know that the last email she sent was to someone about Halloween decorations. Buying some off of someone that posted to Craigslist."

"Did it say what kind of decorations?" Mackenzie asked.

"No. But yeah…I thought the same thing. Creepy dolls would be a pretty popular one these days, don't you think?"

"Where did she meet to get them?"

"I don't know. The seller told her that he would text her to let her know where to meet. And before you ask, we've already checked on the phone. We keep trying to location the phone but it's either dead or turned off."

"I bet the seller…" Ellington said, but stopped himself.

"Go ahead and finish that thought," Mackenzie said. "I was thinking the same thing."

"I bet the seller is the killer. The same jerk that tried to blow my head off."

"I got that hunch, too," Rising said. "But we have no address and no way to trace the phone."

"What about the boyfriend's phone?" Mackenzie asked. "Can you get that? Brian Dixon. If we can get a location on *his* phone, that might lead us to the last place he and Daisy went. Maybe to the selling point for these so-called Halloween decorations."

Rising smiled and pointed at Mackenzie in a child's sort of *bang-bang* salute. "That's a damned good idea. I'll get right on it."

"In the meantime," Mackenzie said, "I want a list of all of the antiques stores, rummage stores, things like that. Maybe even Goodwill stores. I want to find where our killer is getting all of his dolls and dishes. We can use this picture I took at his house to narrow it down."

She showed him the picture and told him about finding the old sticker fragments and sticker residue on many of the dolls and plates. She forwarded him the picture of the sticker she had taken and he looked it over.

"I could get Dentry and Willard on this, but they're already busy. The heroin bust went well last night but we've got several officers tied up with questioning and crime scene investigations. And those agents from the Seattle field office are busy helping with forensics."

"Can you get someone to just start making the list? I can do the calls myself."

"Yes. I'll have you something to work with in half an hour or so."

With that, he left in a hurry, leaving Mackenzie and Ellington in the conference room alone. Mackenzie looked at him as he pored over the case files, trying to force a series of words to her tongue. But as hard as she tried, she could not say what she needed to say. She couldn't even find a way to start.

There's something I need to tell you, she knew she should say. *Something I found out this morning...less than half an hour ago, actually...*

But she couldn't. Not now. Not in the middle of all of this, especially when they seemed to be gaining traction.

The case first, she chided herself. *Personal life second.*

Sure, it was this very line of thought that had led Ellington to describe her to his mother as work-obsessed, but she was okay with that for today. Whether the killer knew it or not, they had him on the run. And while he may feel as if he had the upper hand—basically being a phantom and nearly killing Ellington yesterday—Mackenzie felt that they were actually getting somewhere for the first time since arriving in Seattle. It was a good feeling and she did not intend to lose it.

CHAPTER THIRTY THREE

Mackenzie was starting to like Deputy Rising quite a bit. When the man said he was going to get something done, he did it. Exactly eighteen minutes after heading out to delegate the numerous tasks this case was piling at their feet, he had a receptionist deliver a small list to Mackenzie. There were only eight items on the list, each one the name of a local antiques store or flea market of some kind. According to the receptionist, she'd have at least five or six more for her within a few minutes.

Being that Ellington was still in the room with her, they split the list in half and started calling. It wasn't the most exciting way to get the job done, but it was quick and efficient.

The first call Mackenzie made was to a local thrift store called Threads and Things. The phone was answered by a cheerful older lady. "Threads and Things, this is Alice. Can I help you?"

"Yes ma'am," Mackenzie said. "My name is Mackenzie White, with the FBI. I'm calling because of a local case that may involve certain people buying a very particular item in bulk. And we believe this person is making his purchases at antiques stores or flea markets."

"Oh my. Well, I'll certainly help if I can. What are you looking for, exactly?"

"Dolls and any sort of tea party accessories like a little kid would use. Plastic, porcelain, anything like that. Do you tend to keep that sort of thing there?"

"We do have a few dolls, but they are antiques. We have one from all the way back to 1890. But we've never carried enough to be considered *in bulk.*"

"Okay. And would you mind telling me how you price your items? Do you use stickers, tags, or some other method?"

"When I can, I use tags. I don't like putting stickers on anything—not even DVDs or toys. I hate that sticky residue they leave behind once the customer gets their items home."

"So no stickers at all?"

"No...but, forgive me for asking, but are you specifically *looking* for a place that uses stickers for pricing?"

"I am, actually."

"In that case, you might want to call Mildred Towers. She runs a little operation called Things Forgotten. It's a little like a flea market, but that's sort of complimenting it. It's more like an organized yard sale with a business permit. She's kind of a friend, I guess. I always tell her to stop putting price stickers on her inventory. It looks unprofessional."

"Would you happen to have her information?" Mackenzie asked.

"Somewhere...hold on. I have her business card. She'll sometimes come buy older items that I can't sell. I give them to her at a huge discount just to get them out of my store. And now that I think of it...I'm pretty sure she does have tons of toys. Dolls, action figures, that sort of thing. Ah...here it is."

Alice read Mackenzie the contact information of Mildred Towers, owner of Things Forgotten. "I have to warn you, though," Alice said. "She's only open three days a week and I'm pretty sure today isn't one of them. I don't have her personal number but if you call the number I just gave you, I think her personal information is on her voicemail message."

"Thank you very much, Alice."

"Sure. I hope you find what you're looking for."

Mackenzie ended the call just as Ellington was about to place his second one. "Hold on a second," she said. "I think I might have found what we're looking for. Something sort of like a flea market. Based on what the woman I just spoke with at Threads and Things told me, it's definitely worth checking out."

"Jesus...who names these places?" Ellington asked.

Mackenzie placed the call to Things Forgotten and it went to voicemail, just as Alice from Threads and Things had warned. Mackenzie jotted Mildred Towers's personal number down on the whiteboard, ended the call, and was starting to dial the number when Rising came into the room. He didn't knock this time and he looked excited.

"We got a hit on Brian Dixon's phone," he said.

"At a storage facility?" Ellington asked.

"No. Best we can tell right now is that it's out in the forest on the west edge of the city. And you know as well as I do that can't be good news. You two want to ride over with me to check it out?"

"You guys go," Mackenzie said. "I'm going to follow up on this potential lead. For once, everything seems to be lining up. I don't want to lose the thread."

"If that was a thrift store pun, your game is weak, White," Ellington said, getting to his feet.

"What can I say? When it rains, it pours."

"Terrible," Ellington said.

Mackenzie smiled at him. It was the first genuine smile she had managed in about two days. She and Ellington shared a knowing little grin as he left the room.

You should have told him, she told herself as he left. *You should have told him what you know. The longer you wait, the harder it's going to be...*

For what felt like the millionth time, she pushed that thought away and focused on her phone again. She placed a call to Mildred Towers, feeling that she was slowly coasting up the hill on a roller coaster and the gut-punching drop was coming up any second now, sending her hurtling toward the end of what had so far been a miserable ride.

***

Her drive out to Things Forgotten took Mackenzie back in the direction of Roy's Storage. Mildred Towers had agreed to meet her there at 10:30 to let her have a look around while answering a few questions. The business—if it could be called that—was in a building that looked to have once been a very small diner of some kind. It sat just off of the street, barely allowing enough room for a passable parking lot in front. It was a cute little store but before Mackenzie even stepped inside the building, she could tell that it was going to be something of a mess inside.

She wasn't completely wrong. She saw why Alice from Threads and Things had described it as a mixture of a flea market and yard sale. There was no real organization to the place at all. There were shelves and cases all along every wall of the place. There were cases with used watches and jewelry beside a case stuffed with baseball cards, toy cars, and figurines. An electric guitar hung on the wall with a large sign made out of marker and poster board that read: NAME YOUR PRICE!

There were books and records, clothes and blankets, silverware and electronics. Mackenzie thought it might take an entire day to get a good look at all of the used wares in Things Forgotten.

Still, when she saw Mildred Towers sitting behind a small desk at the back of the central room, the woman looked in good spirits. She even looked rather proud of her little mess as she watched Mackenzie take it all in. She looked to be in her early sixties and regarded Mackenzie from behind a pair of thick glasses.

"Welcome," she said. "It does need some organization, but I also think there's a certain bit of charm to the mess."

"It's certainly a lot to take in," Mackenzie said.

Mildred stood up and walked across the room to shake Mackenzie's hand. "Now, on the phone you said this was an urgent matter. Something to do with someone that might have been a customer. What can I help you with?"

"Well, I'm looking for someone who has sold someone a lot of dolls in the past. Some used, some almost new-looking. Do you sell many dolls?"

"I don't sell many," Mildred said. "I do, however, have a room in the back where I keep things that I have in excess. Quilts, old clothes, even some comic books that I have promised a young man that I would hold onto until he could afford them. At one time, I had boxes upon boxes of dolls. Most of them were old but I did have a few newer ones. And now that you mention it, I did sell most of them to the same customer."

"How about tea sets? Pretend ones, like a little kid might play with."

Mildred looked at Mackenzie as if she'd sensed the question coming. "Yes, I do have some of that sort of stuff. I recently got some new ones in from a woman that was just cleaning out her attic. But yes…I used to keep quite a lot of that sort of stuff here. But the same day I sold all of those dolls, I sold the tea sets, too."

"By any chance, do you remember the customer?"

"Not very well. But I do remember that it was a male. I asked what he needed all of that stuff for and he said he was an artist. That he had some big piece he was working on, like a public art sort of thing."

Mackenzie took out her phone and pulled up the picture she had taken from the killer's house that morning. She showed it to Mildred and asked: "Do you use stickers that look like this on your items?"

"Yes, that's one of mine. I was going to sell the dolls individually, really cheap. But he offered a decent price for several boxes. Same with the tea sets."

"Ms. Towers…I can't stress this enough. Was there *anything* at all that stood out about this man? Anything at all that you could tell me that might help me determine who he is or where he lives?"

Mildred thought about it for a moment, her head cocked as if a memory had just become dislodged. "You know, I think he did make some sort of a comment about the way I had the place set up. He said the mess of it all made him feel claustrophobic. He went on and on about how he hoped it wasn't insulting but he wanted to get out as soon as he could because he was very claustrophobic. He was practically sweating when I led him to the back room where the dolls were."

That checks out with my claustrophobia theory, Mackenzie thought. *Slowly...slowly... We're getting there.*

"Do you remember how he paid?"

"Yes, he paid with cash. And he also…"

Again, she paused here and her face seemed to slowly go pale.

"Ms. Towers?"

"Oh my. Hold on one second, would you, dear?"

Mildred went back behind her little desk and opened up the bottom drawer. She started fishing through it for something, her back bent awkwardly while sitting in the little chair behind the desk.

"People call me a pack rat," she said good-naturedly as she went through the drawer. "I suppose they're right. It's why I love running this little business and maybe why it looks the way it does. But being a pack-rat means I throw nothing away. In this drawer right here, I have messages from clients from years ago. Letters, cards, things like that. I keep it all."

Seconds later, she sat back up. There was a scrap of blue paper in her hand, colored card stock from the looks of it. There was something written on it.

"He left this. I damn near forgot about it. When he was here, I thought I was going to have a woman bring in another tea set that week. I told him and he said he was interested in it. He wanted to know if I could deliver it to him when it came in. And he wanted me to deliver it *here.*"

Mackenzie took the paper and saw that an address had been written on it. *This is it,* she thought. *This is the break we've been waiting for.*

"How long ago was this?"

"Oh, I'm not sure. More than six months ago but certainly not any more than a year. Say eight months ago, just to be safe."

"Did you ever deliver that tea set?"

"No, it never showed up. Besides…there's no way I would have gone out there. A grown man buying several boxes of dolls…I'm not going to just go out in the middle of nowhere and drop some stuff of to him."

"Is that where this is?" Mackenzie asked, showing the address. "The middle of nowhere?"

"Basically. It's a back road that runs along some of those old logging roads that used to run outside of the city back in the forties and fifties."

"Ms. Towers, you've been more help than you can imagine," Mackenzie said. "Thank you so much for your time."

"Of course. Glad to help."

"Do you happen to know how far away this address is?"

"Maybe twenty minutes or so. But I'm telling you, there's not much out there. Seems like the perfect place for a creepy man to go spend some time alone with dolls." She gave a theatric little shiver as she said this.

It was not the image Mackenzie needed in her own mind as she left Things Forgotten, that was for sure. But it was in the center of her mind as she pulled out of the parking lot with the address plugged into her GPS—an address the killer had written in his own handwriting not too long ago.

CHAPTER THIRTY FOUR

"This is Ellington."

Hearing his voice through the phone was just as calming as his arm around her last night when she'd been unable to go back to sleep.

"Where are you right now?" she asked.

"I'm with Rising. We're coming up in the location of Brian Dixon's phone. It's looking like we're going to have to hike a bit out into the woods. How about you?"

"I got a potential address for our killer from the woman at Things Forgotten. I have confirmation that this address was given to her by a man who purchased several boxes of dolls and tea set items all in one fell swoop."

"Mac...you can't go somewhere like that by yourself."

"I'll be fine. She said he purchased the stuff nearly eight months ago. That, plus the fact that he's on the run, makes me think he's not going to be anywhere near a place he considers home. Especially not if he was giving the address to people without any reservation when he was planning all of this."

"Okay," Ellington said, though there was some worry in his voice. "Just be careful. Yesterday proved to me just how quickly things can take a turn for the worst."

"I know. You be careful, too."

She ended the call and checked her GPS again. The route was quickly taking her out of the building and structure of the city, leading into the sparse woodland that sat on the outskirts. Like the rural areas outside of any major city, it started very subtly but, in certain portions, started to overtake the land quickly. According to the route she was seeing, the address wasn't too far away from the house she had already visited twice. This new address was along the same stretch of forest, perhaps eight or nine miles away from the house.

This could be another decoy, she thought. *We've come across two other addresses fairly easily—not to mention a storage unit that he led us directly to. What if this was planned? What if he gave Mildred Towers a fake address just to cover his ass if this day ever came?*

Then she'd have to accept that when the time came. For now, as far as Mackenzie was concerned, it was a hell of a strong lead. Maybe one that would lead them directly to the killer.

CHAPTER THIRTY FIVE

For a moment, she wondered if her GPS had misled her. It wouldn't be the first time it had led her astray in wooded areas. She turned off of the main road and onto a gravel road. This was where the GPS had given up, claiming that she had reached her destination. She nearly turned around when she caught sight of the small turn-off just up ahead. She continued up the gravel road and took the left turn.

She'd been expecting a house, maybe even a mobile home tucked away in the quiet of the woods. But what she saw instead was an old shed. It looked like a hybrid of a barn from a picturesque farm and an older auto garage. There was a single rolling door that took up most of the exterior wall. It was similar to the ones on the storage units she had been investigating, only larger. Beside it was a normal door, battered and discolored with age.

At first glance, the place looked like it hadn't been used for ages. But her GPS had led her here. And it *did* seem like a perfect place to store something as creepy as multiple boxes of dolls. She figured she might as well check it out. She'd driven all the way out here, after all.

She parked her car and stepped out into the little yard area in front of the building. It was quiet here but she could still faintly hear the hum of engines and life six or seven miles to the east where Seattle thrived.

She approached the door slowly. There were four square panes of glass, all stacked two by two to make up a larger square with a cross-shaped pane between them. She peered inside and saw the first indication that maybe the place had been used recently after all. There was a crude little workbench along the back wall. A few tools were scattered around on it. And there, along the back wall, were several boxes.

Mackenzie tried the door, not surprised to find it locked. She looked at the large garage door and wondered if it was even worth trying. She located the handle on the side. It had a lock and a lever mechanism that allowed the user to set the door open at different levels. She grabbed the handle and pulled up hard. The door came up quickly, taking her by surprise. However, it stopped in its tracks after coming up about two feet. There, the rusted latch seemed to catch the progress of the door along the rolling tracks, making it come to a stop. She heaved again, but the door wouldn't budge.

With a sigh, Mackenzie dropped to her knees and then to her stomach. She slid easily under the open space, feeling almost childlike as she rolled under it and into the shed—or garage, or whatever the hell this place was.

She got to her feet, brushing the dirt and dust from her shirt and pants. She started across the large open area toward the boxes but came to a sudden stop.

There was something on the floor—something that made her think of the dream she'd had last night. At first, she thought it was just oil, maybe from someone's truck. But the stuff on the floor was pretty dark. If it was discarded oil, it had only been there for a day or so.

She knelt by the dark liquid on the ground. She touched it gingerly. It was sticky and relatively fresh. She knew right away what it was…had really even known before she had touched it.

It was blood. And a great deal of it.

Mackenzie drew her Glock, suddenly feeling very much trapped. Still, she went to the boxes at the back of the floor. She peered inside the first one and saw several dolls. Her heart hammered in her chest as the entire case seemed to come crashing in around her, all locking into place. There were four other boxes to check. She looked through all of them, finding dolls in all of them and even a few ceramic teapots in the last one.

She then went over to the workbench. There was a soft black mat running along the front of it, the sort to east tension on the ankles and knees from standing for long periods of time. She stepped on this mat as she looked at what was on the bench. There were three screwdrivers sitting there, along with a knife. The knife was gleaming and sparkling clean. One of the screwdrivers, on the other hand, seemed to be coated in blood. Probably the same blood that had been spilled on the floor.

She stepped back off of the mat, fully intending to go back to the car and call Ellington. When she stepped backward, she felt something give underneath the black cushioned mat. She stepped on it again, applying more pressure this time. When she did, she felt more give than the cushion should have supplied.

Mackenzie bent over, grabbed the mat, and pulled it away.

A hatch had been installed in the floor. It made her think that this building had indeed been some sort of garage back in the day. While she had never seen a garage with primitive tools, she was fairly certain this hatch was installed to allow mechanics to get underneath cars when jacks or lifts weren't available.

Unsure of how the hatch even worked, she managed to find a handle at the top, the sort of concave handle that went into the door rather than out like a traditional handle. She grabbed it and pulled it. The door rolled away into a slot that had been installed within the floor, the door sliding back on rusty rails.

She looked down and saw a thin metal ladder attached to a grimy wall. The drop wasn't far at all. She figured she'd probably even have to duck down to fully venture into the space.

"What the hell am I doing?" she asked herself out loud.

She then turned herself around, got on her knees, and started to descend the little ladder. The rungs were cool and grimy, sticky with years upon years of automotive fluids and God only knew what else. When she reached the bottom, she saw that her assumption had been right. The little pit wasn't very deep at all—maybe four feet at most. When Mackenzie stood at full height, the lip of the pit came up to her breasts.

There was a small crawlspace-type area to her right, though. The walls were made of what looked like old boards and plywood. It looked sturdy but still rickety all the same. When she hunkered down, she could just barely make out some gray muted shapes further along the darkened pit. To get back there, she'd have to hunch over severely or even crawl.

She reached for her flashlight, and that's when she heard a voice from overhead.

"You shouldn't have gone down there."

She looked up, fumbling for her Glock as she started to get to her feet.

But she never got into a standing position. The man above her, leering down at her in victory, slammed the door to the pit shut.

The noise was deafening, ringing out like metallic thunder through the pit. With the hatch closed, Mackenzie was thrown into absolute darkness. She instinctually tried pulling at the hatch door, but it did not budge. The man above had apparently locked it.

"You have to let me out," Mackenzie demanded. "I'm an FBI agent. You'll be in a world of shit if you don't me out right now."

The man only laughed. "It seems to me that you're not really in any position to be making demands." He stopped to laugh again and then she could hear his footsteps directly over her.

"My partner will come looking for me," she said.

"Oh, I don't intend for you to be here for long," he said.

"Well, you can't take me to one of your storage units. We've made sure all of them are either closed or under surveillance."

There was a moment's pause before he responded. "Ah, that's fine. I was getting to the end of that, anyway. Running out of places, you know."

There's an admission, Mackenzie thought, doing her best to keep her cool. But she was also unnerved by how casually he spoke. She wondered how much more she could get him to admit to.

"You don't have to do this," she said "Make it easy on yourself. Let me out and we'll figure out how to get you a fair deal."

Again, he laughed. "I think what I've been doing puts any hope of a fair deal well outside of my grasp."

Mackenzie tried to think of the best approach to use to reason with him. He sounded reasonable—of a sound mind. And he was almost boastful in the way he spoke about the things he had done. She wondered if there was a way to use that to her advantage.

While she waited to see what the killer's next move would be, she finally fished out her flashlight. Seeing no sense in causing undue stress on her back and knees, she sat down on the floor of the pit. She turned the flashlight on and pointed it into the dark crawlspace.

And nearly screamed.

There was a body lying about five feet away from her. It had been wrapped in an old tarp, but its legs and its head had come out. A set of dead eyes stared at her, channels of dried blood having cascaded between them down the bridge of the nose. It was a male, somewhere in his mid-twenties. It was a huge guess on her part, but Mackenzie thought this would likely turn out to be Brian Dixon.

"You know…we're at a stalemate here, you and I," he said. "I know you have a gun. But I want to let you out of there. I really do. So what do you suppose we do?"

Mackenzie was listening intently to him, his voice muffled and hollow-sounding through the hatch door. Her world consisted of the little beam of her flashlight and so far all her world contained was herself and a corpse.

She fumbled for her cell phone, managing to dig it out of her pocket with the hand not holding the flashlight. She saw that she had one bar of signal, flickering in and out. She'd had a weak signal the entire way here, but not this bad. She wondered if it was simply being in the building, under the floor. Undeterred, she ignored the signal, hoping for the best. She pulled up her text messages and tapped on the thread with Ellington. She entered the address and added: **In old shed or auto garage. Trapped. Killer is here. Help.**

She pressed send. The progress bar sped ahead at the top of the message and then stopped a third of the way. She stared at it as if willing it to continue, but it remained the same. She placed the phone on the ground at her feet, knowing that she could not distract herself with it.

"You still with me?" he asked from above. "You went quiet. Did you pass out?"

"No. I'm here. And yes, I have a gun. But believe me…my job requires that I try to arrest you—to take you in. I have no intention of shooting you."

"That might be so," he responded. "But I don't know you so I sure as hell don't trust you. I have a better idea. I assume you're here looking for the man that killed all those people…the man that stuck all the bodies in the storage units. What if I told you I could tell you where the newest one is?"

"Her name is Daisy Walker," Mackenzie said. "You killed her boyfriend, Brian Dixon."

"Yeah, that's him down there with you. And honestly, I don't care about their names. Am I supposed to be impressed that you know that much? If you were worth a damn at your job, you would have caught me by now. I mean…I even had to leave you hints to find one of the bodies."

Mackenzie felt rage bubbling up but stomped it down. She had to stay cool and reasonable. He was talking, and that was good. She could buy herself some time. Or, rather, she could buy more time for Ellington to get her text if the fucking thing ever went through.

A thought then occurred to her. Ellington with Rising, locating Brian Dixon's cell phone. If the phone was still *on* Dixon…

She slid over to the body and slowly started to unfold the tarp. The space was tight, so it was difficult but she managed to do it, albeit slowly. While she did so, the killer continued to speak.

"Here's what we'll do. You hand over your gun and I'll tell you where the girl is. I won't lie…she's bleeding. I stabbed her just like the others. Some last a day…some last almost a week. So it's anyone's guess, really. After all…I have a gun, too. Maybe you know the agent who I shot yesterday…"

"You missed," she snapped, unable to keep it in. You were that close and you missed him. He's still very much alive. He's my partner…and all you did was piss him off."

"Sure. Okay."

"You don't believe me?"

He went quiet after this, apparently thinking things over. Mackenzie took that opportunity to continue unfolding the tarp. When the waist of the corpse's pants were exposed, she reached into the pockets. In the front right pocket, she found a wallet. In the back right she felt the familiar rectangular shape of a cell phone. She took it out and pressed the unlock button on the side. While she obviously didn't know the code, she saw all she needed to see. The phone still had fifteen percent of its battery remaining—more than enough to stay alive long enough for Ellington and Rising to triangulate on it.

When the killer finally spoke again, he sounded unusually calm. If he was agitated at her bit of argument, he was hiding it well.

"I'm going to open the hatch," he said. "If you want to know where the girl is, you will hand me your gun, butt first."

"How do I know you won't shoot me?"

"You don't. But I will tell you this: I have the gun on me…the same one I used yesterday. If I wanted to shoot you, I would have done it before trapping you down there."

He probably wants me alive for intel, she thought. *He wants me alive so I can tell him exactly what we know about him.*

"Make your decision, Agent. I'm opening the hatch now."

She heard footfalls and then the clicking of the door beginning to slide open. The hatch was pulled open six inches or so, rays of gritty sunlight coming in and momentarily blinding her.

That's when her text to Ellington went through. She knew it not because she saw it, but because of the tiny sound her outgoing texts made. She always had her notifications set to low volume but in the quiet of the pit, it seemed quite loud.

The hatch door flew open in that moment and suddenly, he was there. "Who the fuck are you texting?"

There was a moment of hesitation as about a million emotions ran the course of the killer's face. But then he raised his gun.

Mackenzie had been ready for it, though. She brought her hand up and fired off a shot just as she pushed herself backward, giving the killer a harder shot. He fired off his shot about half a second after Mackenzie's. Mackenzie was quite sure her shot had missed. As for the killer's shot, it hit the wall about a foot away from where she sat. It sank into the old wooden boards, sending splinters flying.

She saw him looking down at her again and raised her gun. She knew she wouldn't be able to hit him but fired anyway. He jumped back with a yell and slid the hatch back closed. It seemed to snag a bit before it closed but then he slammed it shut with a cry of frustration.

"Congratulations," he screamed. "That girl that's bleeding in a storage unit right now...you just killed her. And as for you...I hope you starve down there."

She heard scurrying footsteps and the sound of things falling over. She had pissed him off and she knew that had been stupid. But when he had angled his gun down at her, she hadn't had a choice. If she hadn't fired at him, he would have probably killed her.

Her...and the baby she was carrying.

The weight of this reality struck her right in the heart and she wanted to fold up and cry in the darkness. Instead, she focused on the sound of the killer's footsteps as he walked away. He slammed the door behind him and left Mackenzie to the silence. She listened for the sound of an engine, wondering where the hell his car had been when she'd arrived. Had he parked behind the building?

She didn't know. And she wasn't going to waste time wondering. She got to her feet as well as she could and waddled over to the ladder. She looked up at the hatch, pointing the flashlight at it. She traced the edges of the hatch's frame and saw where her second shot had struck. It was a small chip on the underside of the frame, almost completely hidden by the closed hatch. She recalled the way the door had snagged when the killer had closed it.

Maybe...

She reached up and found the handle. She dug her fingers into it and pushed hard to the left. Sure enough, it went sliding open. But only several inches. She pushed harder and harder until her fingers and shoulders ached but it would not move any more.

She dug her phone back out and texted Ellington again. **Killer gone. Still trapped. Don't know what he's driving. Block off the main roads, set up a**

But the sound of an engine stopped her. It was not the sound of an engine leaving the building, which was the sound she had expected to hear. Instead, it was *approaching* the building.

But the killer had not left yet. Where the hell was he?

Probably hiding in the same place he was tucked away when you came knocking. And look how easily he snuck up on you.

The sound of the engine came to a stop, followed by the sound of a car door closing. And then a second.

Rising's with him. That's good. This whole thing might end right here...

She almost called out a warning to them but decided not to. No sense in letting the killer know that she was aware someone else had arrived. If he was still there at all, of course. Instead, she deleted everything she had texted before and attempted to start over. But before her fingers could even start the message, she heard a thundering noise as the front door was busted open.

"Mackenzie?"

"Here!" She even stuck her fingers up through the hatch to move the black mat that the killer had placed back over it.

"What the hell?" he said.

His voice was so close and she could not remember ever wanting to see his face so badly. She heard the mat pulled to the side and then saw a sliver of natural light come in through the crack she had managed to open up. She listened to Ellington figure out the latch on the door and then push the door open.

"Are you okay?" he asked.

Hearing him so close made her realize that her ears had been ringing a bit from the close proximity of the three gunshots.

"Yes. I'll catch you up later. I think he's still here somewhere. Maybe out in the woods or hiding behind—"

She was cut off by the sound of a gunshot from outside. And then a second and a third.

"Rising is with you, right?"

"Yeah," Ellington said, drawing his weapon and heading back for the door.

"Careful," she said. "He confirmed that there *is* another woman. She's been stabbed and is bleeding out somewhere in a unit. We can't kill him. He has to tell us where she is."

"Shit." He then went to the door, Mackenzie following behind him. "Rising! Hey, Rising, we can't kill him! He…"

But that's where Ellington stopped. Mackenzie stepped up beside him and peered out the door. She saw the same thing Ellington had seen.

Rising was on the ground in front of their car.

And he wasn't moving.

CHAPTER THIRTY SIX

The thought that had enveloped Mackenzie's entire being while she had been down in the pit seemed to have switched some internal gear within her. *If I put myself at risk, I put the baby at risk…*

So rather than running out to Rising's aid, she fell back into the garage. Ellington took off, though. She watched him go, always impressed with how agile he was. It was like watching some choreographed action movie star on a stage. He strafed his way to the car, keeping his gun level and doing his best to take in the entire scene.

He went to Rising and instantly checked for a pulse. Mackenzie watched it all from the doorway. As Ellington checked on Rising, Mackenzie scanned the immediate area. She could see no sign of the killer. She imagined that after taking down Rising, he had escaped through the forest. Attempted kidnapping of a federal agent and the potential murder of a state policeman could probably spook just about any criminal, no matter how crazy they might be.

She looked back at Ellington and saw that he was saying something to Rising. Surely that was a good sign. Ellington then drew up on his knees and started surveying the area. As he did so, Mackenzie did the only thing she could think to do. She took out her cell phone, not having any sort of mic or radio on her, and placed a call to the Seattle PD. She didn't even allow the woman that answered to get through her introductory spiel.

"This is Agent Mackenzie White, FBI. I've got an officer down with multiple shots fired and a probable suspect in the storage unit murders either pinned down or on the run." She gave the location and ended the call without waiting for confirmation.

Back outside, Ellington was inching his way around the car. She supposed he was going to do the exact same thing she had just done, using the car's radio to call the situation in back at the station. But as he had no idea of where the killer was, his eyes were constantly in motion, trying to take the entire scene in at all at once.

He's an open target out there, she thought. *I have to help. If I go out, I risk the baby. But if I don't, I risk him.*

It was an easier decision than she thought. It literally got her moving as she took her first step outside.

And it was then that she saw him. He was behind the car, tucked down and creeping around the left side, opposite Ellington.

And sensing that Ellington was reaching for the door, the slightest bit distracted, the killer slowly rose, leveling the gun forward while Ellington's head was turned in the opposite direction.

"Down!" she yelled.

Ellington had been trained the same way she had been. When he heard the command from her voice, he fell to the ground with speed and poise. But the killer only jerked hard in her direction, not noticing her. He swung his gun in her direction but didn't have the time to fire off a shot.

Mackenzie's aim was true. She placed one round high in the shoulder. The killer fell backward, catching himself on the side of the car. He was bewildered, but he still held the gun. Mackenzie was prepared to fire again, this time taking out his knee if she had to.

But Ellington had caught on to what was happening. He had been racing around the back of the car following Mackenzie's shot. He tackled the killer to the ground, threw an elbow high into his back, and slapped the gun away. Mackenzie ran out to assist but by the time she reached them, Ellington had already applied a pair of cuffs to the killer's wrists.

They shared a look that spoke volumes. There was so much communicated in it. *I love you. Thanks for saving my life. Damn, that was close. Good job.* And so much more.

"I called it in," Mackenzie said. "We should be good. How's Rising?"

"Looks like a clean shot. Might be too close to his heart, though. I just don't know. He's hanging in there for now."

The killer screamed out in pain as Ellington stood up off of him.

"My shoulder! This fucking hurts!"

"I'm sure it does," Mackenzie said. "Especially with your shoulder pulled back like that because of the cuffs. So…if you tell us where the girl is, we can make it much better."

"Noooo," he bellowed, realizing just how badly the tables had been turned on him.

"You shot a state deputy," Ellington said. "You tried killing me, a federal agent, yesterday. Put that on top of that murders, and things aren't looking good for you. Tell us where the other girl is and make it look a little better."

"Fuck you!" He was writhing now, either from pain or the realization that this was all over for him—that a very bad ending was waiting.

"Is your name Mark Riley?" Ellington asked.

The killer laughed at this while he threw what could only be considered a tantrum. The laugh made it sound like he had some private joke that no one else was in on. And as far as Mackenzie was concerned, that was probably very much the case. Only his joke wasn't funny at all.

"Where's your vehicle?" Mackenzie asked. "I very seriously doubt you walked here."

He said nothing to this, which was as good as a confession. "You good here?" Mackenzie asked Ellington.

"Yeah. You got something?"

"Maybe."

With that, she ran around the side of the building. Around back, there was an old canopy of sorts attached to the garage. It was made of sheet metal and old metal rods. There were several old rotten tires beneath it, along with a gutted dirt bike and assorted car parts. But parked all the way to the right was a car that was much newer than anything else under the canopy. She wasn't sure of the year or exact model, but it was a Ford Taurus, no older than 2005 for sure.

She went to the driver's side door and opened it. The keys weren't in the ignition and there were no obvious signs of ownership. She reached in and popped open the glove compartment. A few things came spilling out, fast food napkins and condiment packets among the mess. But then she saw something that caught her attention. A little flash of bright yellow. She reached for it and knew what she had found before she pulled it out.

The yellow was a strip of tape that had been placed on top of a key. Just like they had seen for the smaller units at Roy's Storage. The key was attached to a key ring with several other keys. Without doing a hard count, she was sure there were at least ten on the ring. One of them was tagged with a small plastic tab that read **Unit C4 – U-Store-It.**

She took the keys and ran back to the car. Ellington was holding his gun on the killer, a man she assumed was not really named Mark Riley at all. She was thinking he just used it as a moniker, a way to confuse people if he ever got caught. And it sure as hell had worked for a while.

He was sitting against the side of the car now, the wound in his shoulder bleeding lightly through his shirt. He looked a little scared when he saw that Mackenzie was carrying his ring of keys.

"I can clearly see that one was from Roy's Storage and another is from U-Store-It. Only, the one at U-Store-It wasn't your unit. It belonged to one of your victims. How did you happen to get it?"

"You're the FBI agent. You figure it out."

"We've got the keys," she said. "It might take a few hours, but we'll find her. Do one decent thing and tell us where she is. Give her a chance to live."

"Why?"

And it was that one simple question, along with the deadened look in his eyes, that told Mackenzie that there was trauma there. He was doing these horrific things because of some past hurt, some event that had so badly scarred him that this was how he had chosen to work it out. But even that realization did not humanize him. She thought of him leering down at her, just a thought away from killing her and her unborn child.

She thought of those poor women, bleeding and suffering and starving in those units. Alone, afraid, cast aside like trash.

The sound of approaching sirens broke those thoughts apart. She stood directly next to Ellington and took his hand. "When they get here, I want to let the police take him in. I can't be here. I can't be around him much longer. I want to go find Daisy Walker."

"We can do that," he said.

The sirens got louder and within another minute or so, the flashing lights of an ambulance came down the gravel road. Several cop cars fell in behind it.

The killer looked at it all as if he were in a dream. He then looked at the agents, almost as if he was expecting them to explain what was happening.

"Last chance," Mackenzie said. "Her name is Daisy Walker. You killed her boyfriend. Her mother is worried about her. Do one thing decent."

He only shook his head. The ambulance came into the little pull-over that served as the old garage's parking lot. When two police cars came to shuddering stops behind it, that was all it took. Mackenzie gave the killer one last glance and then headed for her car with the keys in her hand. She thumbed through them all, wondering which one was going to reveal Daisy Walker, wondering which key might very well save her life.

157

CHAPTER THIRTY SEVEN

Mackenzie had told the killer that she guessed they'd find the unit that Daisy Walker was in within a few hours. But as it turned out, with eight policemen working along with her by calling and visiting storage facilities, they were able to narrow it down to two potential sites in less than one hour. They used the type of key cut as well as identifying marks on each key to narrow it down. Both of the owners had willingly closed their gates when the police had asked the day before, so they seemed more than happy to help. The prospect of no longer inconveniencing their customers and the risk of losing money was more than enough reason to rapidly help the police.

Dentry, the officer who had been alongside Rising for parts of the case, had been the one to eliminate a place called, uncreatively, A Place for Your Stuff. There was indeed a unit rented to Mark Riley. The owner nervously checked the unit out over the phone and found it untouched.

Mackenzie and Ellington were on their way to the PD to speak with the killer as soon as they could when they got the update. Dentry made the call, informing them over Mackenzie's phone, which she had set to speaker mode.

"That leaves only one place," Dentry said. "A place called X-tra Space. It's out near Redmond, about twenty minutes away. We've tried calling the owner but there's no answer."

"We're already out and have the keys," Mackenzie said. "We'll take it. Thanks, Officer Dentry. Make sure to get an ambulance out there, too."

"I'll make sure it's done right away."

"Any word on Rising?"

"No. Nothing. All we know is he's stable, but just barely."

"Has the killer talked yet?" Ellington asked.

"I don't think so. He's just been checked into the hospital for the gunshot wound. When everyone heard about what happened to Rising, one of our officers that took him to the hospital took a swing at him and spit in his face. It was a real circus. Should we wait for you before anyone questions him?"

"No," Mackenzie said. The thought of being alone in a room with him made her angry and a bit uneasy. But then, she realized that with Rising out of commission, she and Ellington were the most obvious choice. She certainly couldn't let the local field agents interrogate him. "Actually, yes. Please let us get first crack at him. Give us an hour or two, okay?"

"Sounds good." And it really did seem that's how Dentry felt. There was relief in her voice. She'd wanted no part of the man who had killed at least four and might have been successful and claiming the life of a fifth.

That would actually be eleven in all if he was also responsible for the murders in Salem, Oregon, too.

It was a sobering thought for sure. And it made her feel all the more relieved when they arrived at X-tra Space twenty-two minutes later. Ellington was driving and when he pulled into the parking lot from the street, the car fishtailed from the speed. There was no gate or locked entrance, but Mackenzie did see three tall utility poles on the premises with security cameras.

"So where the hell do we start?" Ellington asked as they got out of the car and rushed to the units.

"With the smaller ones," Mackenzie said, pointing to the left, near the back side of the property.

There were eight smaller units located at the back of the property. With no other way to eliminate them, Mackenzie had no choice but to try them all one at a time, inserting the key from the killer's ring into each lock and trying, hoping it would unlock.

The key did not turn until the fifth unit. The key turned fully, rewarding them with a faint *click* as it disengaged. Ellington pulled the door up quickly, the sound of it like a screeching robot.

Mackenzie had expected a dead body. She'd expected lots of blood and a warm yet lifeless body.

So when the young woman on the concrete floor actually craned her neck up at them and started screaming tiny muffled noises through the gag around her mouth, Mackenzie's heart swelled. And damn it, she couldn't help it; she started to cry.

There was indeed lots of blood, but Mackenzie managed to look beyond that. She held eye contact with Daisy Walker, not looking at the stab wound high in her stomach, not looking around the unit to see if there were any dolls or tea party decorations.

"You're okay, sweetie," Mackenzie said. "We've got you."

As she did her best to calm Daisy, Ellington removed the gag and the wire that had been bound around her arms. She started to scream in pain—cries so deep and with breaths so ragged that Mackenzie feared she might pass out.

Again, the sound of approaching ambulance sirens sent a flood of relief through her. They were very close, the wails of the sirens

159

growing quickly. Mackenzie remained on the floor of the unit and took Daisy's hand. Her grip was weak and there were tremors running through her body. But at least she was alive. Mackenzie decided to focus on that fact as the wailing sirens drew closer and Daisy Walker trembled and struggled to stay alive beside her.

CHAPTER THIRTY EIGHT

They followed the ambulance through a mist of rain. Something about the final stages of a case taking place in a hospital was unnerving to Mackenzie but based on the way this case had gone, it seemed almost fitting. They entered the hospital with far too many question marks for Mackenzie to rest comfortably on the day's success. Deputy Rising was now listed as officially stable, but he had at least two surgeries in his future to repair the damage from the shot that had torn through his chest, missing his heart by less than two inches.

As for Daisy Walker, the paramedics had not been hopeful. When they placed her in the back of the ambulance, Daisy had finally given in and passed out. Her pulse had been incredibly weak and she had been non-responsive. And that was the last that Mackenzie had seen or heard of the young woman's fate.

As Mackenzie and Ellington walked toward the hospital lobby elevators, Dentry came running up to them. She'd apparently been sitting in the waiting area, wanting to grab them as soon as they came in.

"The doctors cleared the suspect for interrogation about five minutes ago," Dentry said. "The shot was clean and they fixed it up quickly. As soon as he was given the okay, the suspect asked to talk to Agent White."

"Me specifically?" she asked.

"Not by name. He asked to speak with the agent that found him—the agent he trapped down in the dark. That was how he put it."

"Where is he?"

"You don't have to do what he says," Ellington said.

"It's okay. I want to. I think I need to." What she didn't say, but was thinking, was: *I need to understand.*

"Second floor, in a secured room," Dentry said.

Dentry got on the elevator with them and took it up to the second floor. Mackenzie instantly saw the police guard stationed outside of a room near the end of the hallway. She wasted no time in heading that way.

"Mac," Ellington said softly as they approached. "Don't push yourself. If he starts getting to you, you come out and—"

She stopped him here by stepping close to him. She gave him a small hug, not caring that Dentry was right there beside them. She lightly kissed him on the side of the head, just below his earlobe, and whispered in his ear. "I'm pregnant."

She wasn't sure why she chose that moment to tell him. It seemed like those two words almost answered any questions he had about why she felt the need to speak with the killer. She had to understand. She had to get a better understanding of men that did evil and atrocious things if she was going to bring a child into this world.

When she pulled back, Ellington was clearly shocked. But there were the faintest traces of a smile at the corner of his mouth. "Yeah?" he said.

She smiled and nodded. And without saying another word, she went into the suspect's hospital room.

***

"The doctor says you're a good shot," the killer said as she walked into the room. He was sitting on the edge of a hospital bed with his right arm handcuffed to the rail. "He said it was a perfectly clean shot that could have killed me if it had strayed four inches or so further down."

She ignored this and took a seat in the visitor's chair. "Officer Dentry said you wanted to talk to me."

"I do. I wanted to know how you found me."

"I want to know your name. Your real name. Not Mark Riley."

He smiled and shook his head.

"It doesn't matter. We have your car. We'll have it soon."

"It doesn't matter."

"The dolls," Mackenzie said. She recalled the way he had freely talked when he'd had her trapped. Maybe she could coerce him into slipping up and revealing more than he intended. "I figured out where you purchased them from. And the woman that owns the place had kept the address you gave her." She considered something for a moment and then added: "Did you know what you were going to do when you bought them?"

"I had the idea in my head."

"Why do it?" Mackenzie asked. She felt herself beginning to get emotional but used every ounce of willpower within her to keep it down. She was not going to let this man see her cry.

"I wish I could tell you. It was cathartic. All of it. The abductions, the wounding, knowing that I had caused someone to suffer...to die slowly. And as I say it...yes, I understand how messed up and twisted it sounds. But it...it helped."

"And the dolls and the tea party?"

He seemed to think about this for a moment but then shook his head. He looked at her with a bit of a sneer. "That's private," he said.

"You were in Salem, Oregon, too, right?" Mackenzie asked. "That brings your total to ten. That's right...ten. Daisy Walker would have been eleven, but we found her in time. No thanks to you."

"I wanted to talk to you because you were down there...down in the dark, in the pit," he said. "And you handled it well. It seemed not to bother you. How did you do it?"

She wasn't sure what sort of answer he was looking for. She could easily recall being down there, stranded and alone in the dark (well, not entirely alone if you counted Brian Dixon's dead body).

"How did *you* do it?" Mackenzie asked. "How did you end these lives and cause so much pain and death and not care?"

"You don't think I cared?" he asked, as if offended. "Oh, I cared a great deal. But...like I said: It was the only thing that helped."

"Helped what?"

He got that angry look in his eyes again. It almost made him look like a frustrated child who could not get his way. "That's private," he said again.

As Mackenzie tried to think of some other way to get answers from him, there was a knock at the door. She saw Ellington there, beckoning her outside. She left the killer and joined Ellington and Dentry in the hallway. There were two others with them now, one man and one woman, dressed in a way that made Mackenzie assume they were the local field agents. Middle-of-the-line suits that looked a little too casual to be high end.

"These are Agents Smith and Gonzalez," Ellington said. "They just got a call with just about everything we could need to know about the suspect."

"It just took tracing down his car registration and plates," the man said, his mildly Hispanic complexion making Mackenzie assume he was Agent Gonzalez.

"And it's not pretty," Smith said. She read from her phone, apparently either a text or email that had just been sent directly to her. "Suspect's name is Aiden Childress. Born in Sacramento, California, where, at the age of eight, he was placed into foster care after his mother was sentenced to time in a mental institution after

163

being found guilty of killing her daughter. The daughter was five years old at the time and she died right in front of Aiden. An investigation showed that the mother poisoned the water they were using to have little pretend tea parties. During the trial, she claimed she only intended to make her daughter sick enough to continue getting government assistance for medical bills.

"But it wasn't the first time she'd been in trouble for such a thing. The father, a year previous, had been arrested for child neglect and child abuse. Both children were found locked inside dog crates while the father was doing drugs in the bedroom with a woman that was not his wife. A legal battle for custody ensued, as the mother worked hard to keep her children from going into the system. She won, but it only lasted a year. That's when she killed her daughter."

"Anywhere in there indicate that Aiden Childress ever lived in or around Salem, Oregon?" Mackenzie asked.

Smith scanned the message and stopped after a few seconds, clearly shocked. "Yes, actually. I've got records of parking tickets and a permanent residence for a period of about eight years."

Mackenzie looked back into the room and saw Aiden Childress, still sitting on the edge of the bed. He had a very patient look on his face, one that seemed to be studying his surroundings and taking it all in while he waited for Mackenzie to return.

But she wasn't going back in there. Agents Smith and Gonzalez had found the answers she had been looking for. And sadly, it was something she had seen far too many times. The evil in the hearts of men didn't just materialize overnight. Far too often it was almost genetic, passed down through traumas and violent events the same as a likelihood of male pattern baldness or a tendency toward alcoholism.

But she recalled being down in that pit and how Childress had looked down into it. And then his comments moments ago: *You handled it well. It seemed not to bother you. How did you do it?*

Picturing him as a young boy locked in a dog crate made the question make more sense. And sadly, so did his little games with the dolls and the tea party. And despite all that she had seen in the storage units, the most telling scene had been in the doghouse out by his house. Those dolls, sitting around eternally, waiting for someone to come to their tea party.

It sent a chill through her...one that remained and turned into goosebumps. And once more, she felt herself on the edge of tears.

"Thanks, Agents," she said. "Would you mind beginning to process him? When you do, make a formal request to have records pulled from Salem, Oregon, for similar murders."

"Absolutely," Gonzalez said.

With that, Mackenzie started down the hall. She felt Ellington fall in beside her and that meant the world to her. He took her hand and they went to the second-floor waiting room at the end of the hall. There, they sat down together and Ellington drew her close. She wept against his shoulder and it felt good to finally let it out.

She was going to be a mother. She was going to bring life into a world where parents mistreated their children—where those same children grew up to commit senseless acts in an effort to make sense of their pasts. It was mostly an evil world…something that Mackenzie had not really believed before. She'd always tried to see the good in it all but it was damned hard after meeting someone like Aiden Childress face to face.

But she knew there was good. That there was light in the darkness. It came in unexpected ways sometimes, like taking a pregnancy test in a convenience store bathroom and having your life forever changed.

"So you're pregnant, huh?" Ellington said as her sobs died down.

"Yeah."

And to prove once again that he knew her well, inside and out, his next comment not only set her at ease, but reminded her of why she loved him so fiercely.

"In that case, do you mind if we wait to have the wedding when you're like eight months along and really showing? It'll make my mother insane."

CHAPTER THIRTY NINE

She'd heard about morning sickness from movies, TV shows, and a few friends back in Nebraska, so Mackenzie had been expecting the worst. But hitting the nine-week mark following her first OB visit, she hadn't experienced it at all. She was suffering from pretty severe mood swings, which at least explained her behavior in Seattle. But back in DC, the mood swings got slightly worse. Partly because she was back in the part of the world where her upcoming wedding was a hot topic and partly because Ellington was so excited about their recent turn of events.

At work, she kept tabs on how things were turning out back in Seattle with the Aiden Childress case. Five days after they returned home, she received a call from Rising. He had one surgery still scheduled but was doing well. He was back at home but would not be able to return to work for at least another three months.

She learned all of this one day after lunch, sitting in her office. Rising had called her cell phone and when she saw his name on the display, she'd answered right away with a smile. He'd filled her in as best he could and gave his sincere thanks for the way she and Ellington had wrapped the case.

"But I didn't call to talk about me," Rising said. "I thought you'd want to know that Daisy Walker is going to pull through. The wound to her stomach caused some intestinal damage and she lost a lot of blood. Those two things together resulted in a nasty infection, but as of this morning, the doctors are saying things look quite promising."

"That's great news," Mackenzie said. "Do we know anything new about Aiden Childress?"

"He's been officially arrested and right now is being held in the secure wing of a maximum security prison. I haven't talked much about it with anyone, but from what I understand, he'd likely get some sort of psychiatric flexibility when it comes to his trial. Based on his history…"

"Yeah, I expected that."

"Anyway…again, thanks so much for your help. I do need to warn you that Mrs. Shelby Walker is dying to get your number. She's incredibly grateful that you were able to save her daughter."

She thought of Mrs. Walker and how she had sat like a sentinel on her porch, waiting for news of her daughter. It was a thought that made Mackenzie look down to her stomach—still flat and looking perfectly normal—with a smile. And although things with Aiden Childress had gotten darker and darker the more they learned about his past, the possibilities growing within her made Mackenzie start to think that there was more light and promise in the world than she had originally thought.

***

In the dream, she was in the pit again. Her flashlight was on but its light was red. As she traced the shape of the pit, she saw dolls lined up against the walls. And there, against the back, a bassinet that was overflowing with blood.

A voice whispered in her ear as a hand caressed her shoulder. "You think you can really handle that?"

She turned and saw her father sitting in the darkness with her, his face painted in that same red light. But he was not dead or injured or bleeding the way he had been in all of the previous dreams she'd had about him. He was perfectly fine. He was smiling at her and his touch on her shoulder was reassuring.

"I think I can, Dad. Yes, I do."

"Then do it," he said. "Get your ass out of this darkness and do it."

Mackenzie awoke with a start. She sat up in bed and looked around the room. The whisper of her father's voice was still in her mind and it made her miss him for the first time in a long time.

"You okay?" Ellington murmured from beside her in bed.

"Yeah. Just a dream."

"Bad one?"

"Not too bad. Maybe even good."

He rolled over and gently placed his hand on her stomach. "Good. You deserve a few of those from time to time."

She lay back down with his hand still on her stomach. He'd been doing that a lot lately, on the couch while watching TV, in bed, passing each other in the kitchen.

As selfish as it seemed, she thought he was right. They both deserved to have good dreams on occasion. Because if all there was to be had were bad dreams, what did that say about the world?

She closed her eyes again, resting her hand on top of Ellington's. She drifted off with a head full of hopes and dreams for the life being created beneath their hands.

NOW AVAILABLE!

BEFORE HE LAPSES
(A Mackenzie White Mystery—Book 11)

From Blake Pierce, #1 bestselling author of ONCE GONE (a #1 bestseller with over 1,200 five star reviews), comes BEFORE HE LAPSES, book #11 in the heart-pounding Mackenzie White mystery series.

BEFORE HE LAPSES is book #11 in the bestselling Mackenzie White mystery series, which begins with BEFORE HE KILLS (Book #1), a free download with over 500 five-star reviews!

FBI Special Agent Mackenzie White, six months pregnant, calls off her formal wedding with Ellington and they elope instead. On their honeymoon, they finally have some downtime together—when a call comes in for an urgent case: women are being strangled at a rapid rate in the D.C. area by what appears to be a serial killer. Even more disturbing: this killer is so meticulous that he leaves absolutely no trace.

Mackenzie comes up with a radical theory for who he might be, but pursuing it may jeopardize her own job—and her own life. In her most intense game of cat and mouse yet, she finds herself struggling to keep her baby and her sanity while up against a diabolical psychopath, her own agency, and the hunt of her life.

Even with her all of her wits, it may be too late for her to save the next victims—or herself.

A dark psychological thriller with heart-pounding suspense, BEFORE HE LAPSES is book #11 in a riveting new series—with a beloved new character—that will leave you turning pages late into the night.

Also available by Blake Pierce is ONCE GONE (A Riley Paige mystery—Book #1), a #1 bestseller with over 1,200 five star reviews—and a free download!

Blake Pierce

Blake Pierce is author of the bestselling RILEY PAGE mystery series, which includes thirteen books (and counting). Blake Pierce is also the author of the MACKENZIE WHITE mystery series, comprising nine books (and counting); of the AVERY BLACK mystery series, comprising six books; of the KERI LOCKE mystery series, comprising five books; of the MAKING OF RILEY PAIGE mystery series, comprising two books (and counting); of the KATE WISE mystery series, comprising two books (and counting); and of the CHLOE FINE psychological suspense mystery, comprising two books (and counting).

An avid reader and lifelong fan of the mystery and thriller genres, Blake loves to hear from you, so please feel free to visit www.blakepierceauthor.com to learn more and stay in touch.

BOOKS BY BLAKE PIERCE

CHLOE FINE PSYCHOLOGICAL SUSPENSE MYSTERY
NEXT DOOR (Book #1)
A NEIGHBOR'S LIE (Book #2)

KATE WISE MYSTERY SERIES
IF SHE KNEW (Book #1)
IF SHE SAW (Book #2)

THE MAKING OF RILEY PAIGE SERIES
WATCHING (Book #1)
WAITING (Book #2)

RILEY PAIGE MYSTERY SERIES
ONCE GONE (Book #1)
ONCE TAKEN (Book #2)
ONCE CRAVED (Book #3)
ONCE LURED (Book #4)
ONCE HUNTED (Book #5)
ONCE PINED (Book #6)
ONCE FORSAKEN (Book #7)
ONCE COLD (Book #8)
ONCE STALKED (Book #9)
ONCE LOST (Book #10)
ONCE BURIED (Book #11)
ONCE BOUND (Book #12)
ONCE TRAPPED (Book #13)
ONCE DORMANT (book #14)

MACKENZIE WHITE MYSTERY SERIES
BEFORE HE KILLS (Book #1)
BEFORE HE SEES (Book #2)
BEFORE HE COVETS (Book #3)
BEFORE HE TAKES (Book #4)
BEFORE HE NEEDS (Book #5)
BEFORE HE FEELS (Book #6)
BEFORE HE SINS (Book #7)
BEFORE HE HUNTS (Book #8)
BEFORE HE PREYS (Book #9)

BEFORE HE LONGS (Book #10)

AVERY BLACK MYSTERY SERIES
CAUSE TO KILL (Book #1)
CAUSE TO RUN (Book #2)
CAUSE TO HIDE (Book #3)
CAUSE TO FEAR (Book #4)
CAUSE TO SAVE (Book #5)
CAUSE TO DREAD (Book #6)

KERI LOCKE MYSTERY SERIES
A TRACE OF DEATH (Book #1)
A TRACE OF MUDER (Book #2)
A TRACE OF VICE (Book #3)
A TRACE OF CRIME (Book #4)
A TRACE OF HOPE (Book #5)

43145967R00099

Made in the USA
Middletown, DE
20 April 2019